The Crusade's Secrets

Fanny Garstang

Chapter 1

Spring 1100

For most of the return journey, by ship and then overland, it had been uncomfortable for Constance and her growing belly. They were therefore both thankful to their hosts, the Fouquets, for allowing them to stay for Constance's last month of pregnancy. It had been with relief that the elderly knight and his wife had welcomed them into their home. Although they were in Normandy they hadn't gone to family for fear of the reaction. Madame Fouquet had insisted on the couple staying when she saw how far advantaged Constance's pregnancy was.

A week before the child was due they persuaded the local priest to bless them in the Fouquet's small solar. Even though they had had sex neither had considered themselves married until they realised Constance was pregnant. Pierre wanted their marriage to be recognised by the church so that there wouldn't be any protest if the baby was a boy and therefore the heir. With the elderly couple as their witnesses the priest blessed them. The priest didn't seem overly impressed by the fact they had been to the Holy Lands.

Constance wore early spring flowers plaited into her hair while her dress had been expanded to allow for the baby's growth and her enlarged breasts. In Pierre's eyes, after the first trimester of throwing up, Constance had bloomed. She gave him a tight smile as he placed a ring on her wedding finger.

The baby was an active one in its womb and she felt it kick hard against her insides. It felt painful to Constance and as she placed a hand on her swollen stomach she turned to Madame Fouquet, an experienced mother of seven grown children, "Is it beginning?"

Going to her side the lady placed a hand on Constance's stomach as well, "I cannot be sure. It may just be moving round to ready itself. If it is a strong child it may be wanting to come out sooner rather than later. We will see how it goes. It may be a few days yet or it maybe later on today. It is God's will when it happens. We will just have to wait. To be on the safe side you'd probably best retire."

They all looked to the priest for permission to leave. He scathingly remarked, "it seems we were just in time." For that comment he received a glare from the lady of the manor and retorted, "have you ever seen the Holy Lands and saved them from the Mohammeds?" He scowled at her before stalking out of the room.

It was later that night as they were both in their wedding bed that Constance felt a cramp go down her spine to her womb. She clutched at her stomach and moaned. She felt the child kick at the top of her stomach as if it was going to kick its way out of her as fast as possible. It was then she felt wetness between her thighs and soaking into the bed sheets. She whispered fearfully to Pierre, "I think the baby is coming." With fear growing in her voice, "Oh Lord, please keep me well. Pierre… Oh!"

There was another weak spasm, one of many that would grow in intensity and frequency as the labour progressed.

"I will get Mistress Fouquet. She will know what to do." Pierre responded as he threw back the bedcovers.

Madame Fouquet followed Pierre back to the chamber with a tallow light in one hand and the other clutching the corners of a blanket she had wrapped round herself against the night's chill air. As soon as she appeared Constance felt calmer and more confident and that everything was going to turn out fine. The old lady placed a warm hand on Constance's belly, "It will be a few hours yet. Hopefully he is the right way round which will make it an easy birth."

"He? Right way round?" Constance queried with fear.

"How do you know it is a he?" Pierre demanded.

"It is just something, a feeling, dear after the number of births I have had and seen in this house. Now put a log on that fire and then go and get one of the girls to help me." Madame Fouquet instructed him without turning her attention away from the young mother-to-be.

The sun was rising pink in the eastern sky when Constance pushed out a dark haired head. Her hair was plastered to her skin from sweat. She gasped for breath before her face screwed up with another urge to push. It was then that the baby slipped out with a wail from its blood stained body. For a moment it was the only sound in the room until all three women recovered from the shock of another child entering the world. Through gasps, before her body demanded her to push out the afterbirth, Constance looked to Madame Fouquet, "Is it a he?"
The other woman gathered the bloody child in an old woollen blanket and wiped the blood from its naked body while Madame Fouquet cut through the umbilical cord. The two Norman women examined the child which was now whimpering, "You have a boy."
"Is he healthy?"

"Why ask such a silly question as you have already heard his hearty cry." Madame Fouquet smiled with amusement. She helped Constance off the birthing stool and wiped her down and then got her into the newly laid bed. She kept hold of the babe as the new mother hesitated in holding him.

"Is it safe to come in?" The jolly host peered round the door, "I hear a baby's cry."

"Send the father in." Madame Fouquet replied.

Pierre appeared looking nervous, "well?" Stepping into the room he was hit by the smell of sweat, blood and burnt herbs in the fire's embers.

"We have a son." Constance said with a tired smile from the bed, "what should we call him?"

"David." Was Pierre's instant reply while trying to decide where to look first, his wife or his new son.   "Is that wise?"

"What do you mean? What is wrong with naming him after my brother?" He frowned.

"It doesn't feel right?" She carefully replied.

"What do you want to call him then?" Pierre responded with irritation.

"I don't know, let me think about it." She said as her eyes began to close.

Spotting that Constance needed to sleep Madame Fouquet hustled the two men from the room. As her eyes closed Constance began to wonder if the baby was actually Pierre's. A part of her wondered if it belonged to another man, David, due to the timing of the birth. She decided at that point never to let Pierre know of her uncertainty. It would be best to let Pierre believe it was his son especially as he had never noticed that she was not a virgin when he had first slept with her back in Jerusalem.

A few days later the child was baptised just in case the boy suddenly died, though by his crying it seemed he had no desire to just yet. Standing by the font Constance knew what she was going to call the little boy. She decided to keep

Pierre happy as she leant against him. The priest held the once again wailing infant as he waited for the parents to give him a name for the newborn before he was dipped in the font of Holy water. Constance said, "In respect to the family that has brought me up…?"

"How about Pascal as it is the time of Easter?" The priest suggested as he saw Constance hesitate.

"Yes, Pascal, father. That is an appropriate name for this time of year." She smiled with relief. She had momentarily dithered in calling the boy either after Sir Henri or her own deceased father. She glanced at Pierre and saw that he didn't look as happy but it was now too late as the priest had dipped the baby's head in the font. Pierre glowered and was the first to leave the church. He had really wanted David as the name to his son and now it had been forfeited for a completely different name. He wasn't going to let Constance off that one. He would find some way to punish her for changing the name at the last minute.

Pierre's feet had become so itchy to move on that two weeks later they had to leave the Fouquets' welcoming hearth. It was with tears and hugs that they left the yard. Owen, their manservant since the beginning of the Crusade, led Constance's horse on a rope while she sat astride it with baby Pascal wrapped up against her chest against the spring's cool air.

Pierre didn't want to wait any longer then he had to in telling his parents of David's death. Constance had appeared to have accepted David's death far easier than Pierre but that was a front. Inside, though she wouldn't tell him so, she thought David still lived. Her emotional heart wouldn't let her believe David was dead, just as Pierre had once thought. She knew David had been sensible and only in the worst situation would he have got himself killed. She felt that if they went back now, to Jerusalem, they would find him alive and well and welcoming them with a ready smile and open arms.　　　Constance stopped her horse when Renard Manor came into view, down the track, even though it was raining. Behind her stood the wooden rectangular building of the church yet to be converted into stone. At the junction her horse stood as was the village barn where all the taxed food was stored. The manor building with its whitewashed wattle and daubed hall on a foundation of stone hadn't changed.

　　Pierre glanced behind and saw she had stopped. He stopped his own horse and asked, "What are you looking at?" "The house. It has been a long time since I've seen it and it doesn't look like its changed at all."

　"It has been four years." He agreed softening briefly though he was eager to be out of the saddle, "come on though; we are nearly there."

　"I don't think I can do this Pierre."

He frowned, "what do you mean?"

　"I don't want to see Aunt Lucille's face or even Uncle Henri's at that when we tell them about Davy."

　"I'm not expecting you to tell them. They are my parents so I will tell them. Come on, I don't know about you but I'm feeling saddle sore and I'm sure the horses are fed up of carrying us and our earnings. At least they will be pleased to see us at first especially as we have Pascal to show them." He gave her a tight smile, "Ready now?"

　　They entered the hall with both wondering why no one had appeared to greet them but then again outside it was pouring with rain. Sir Henri and Lady Lucille's eyes widened and both got to their feet at the sight of the wet Pierre and Constance and baby. Neither could find their voices for a moment but Lady Lucille's eyes were flicking round. She could see one son and Constance with a baby. Rapidly her breathing became heavier and her bosom heaved. Her voice came out quiet and afraid,

"Where is Davy?"

Sir Henri took hold of his wife and guided her to her armless chair and decided not to reprimand her on the childhood name of their younger son as he looked to his eldest,

"Pierre?"

A sob came from Lady Lucille and she covered her face to hide the tears. Her shoulders shook and her husband rested a hand on one of them. Pierre looked solemnly at his father,

"He died rescuing the Holy City."

"At least it was there and not at the beginning. Is he buried properly so that he can go to Heaven?"

Pierre and Constance glanced at each other and then he lied, a white lie, "Yes."

"Good."

"He's not dead." Lady Lucille suddenly exclaimed and she looked fiercely at her eldest.

"Mother, I believed that also but now I have come to accept that he has gone." Pierre said with fear that she would become mad from grief.

"All of you have a place in my heart and David's piece does not feel empty like it would be if he was dead." She returned firmly, "He lives I am sure." She said it with so much confidence that even Sir Henri felt concerned for his wife's sanity. He crouched down at her side, "Lucille, don't make this any harder then it already is. I don't want to believe it but I am going to have to and so are you."

"I can't though." She protested though the tears continued to fall, "maybe you didn't bury him, maybe... maybe he is alive and well and out there still. Are you sure it was him you buried and not some other poor soul?"

Constance passed Pascal to Owen who clumsily held him while she went to the woman who had cared for her most of her life and put her arms round her. Lady Lucille frowned and demanded, "Where have you been? Why are you all brown from the sun? You could have let us know where you have been. Whose is the child?" "He is ours." Pierre responded, puffing out his chest in pride of his strong healthy son.

"Pierre?" His mother looked at him, "Constance?" Lady Lucille exclaimed, "You know you weren't supposed to go with them to the Holy Lands. We have been worrying for you and believed you were dead or even drowned crossing the sea back to us."

"But I'm not am I? Anyway there were other women and even children with us." Constance said in defence.

"We told you that you weren't to go and you should have obeyed. How are you to marry if you can't be obedient?" Constance looked to Pierre since the question had come up. Though he had wanted to wait a few days it seemed it wasn't going to happen. He stepped forward, "Mother we are married so that Pascal would be born in wedlock."

Though they could have celebrated none of them were really in the mood to. They went to bed early. Unable to sleep Constance crept from the bedroom that Pierre and she was now sharing with Pascal in a cradle at the foot of the bed, and was surprised to find her aunt still up and looking into the central dying fire. Cautiously she crossed to the woman and knelt in the rushes at Lady Lucille's feet, "Aunt Lucille, I believe you. I'm sure he is alive as well."

"But you could not convince Pierre the same." The elder woman stated mournfully.

"At the beginning when we first began to realise he believed David was alive but overnight it changed and I was the one to believe while he thought David dead. I tried but it didn't work."

"Stubborn like his mother." Lady Lucille remarked with a tight smile.

"What should we do aunt?"

"Let it be for the time being. Perhaps David was injured and is already making his way home. Pierre's lying has not improved and you can't hide anything from a mother. You did not bury him did you?"
Constance bowed her head in shame, "we could not find him amongst the dead."

"Is it true that Pascal is Pierre's?" Lady Lucille demanded.

"Yes. He was conceived at Jerusalem." She answered simply, refraining from explaining how or why it had happened.
Lady Lucille looked to her adopted daughter, "You should go to bed Constance and try and sleep."

"What about you aunt?"

Lady Lucille gave her a small smile, "I'll go to bed as well now. I just needed a little time to myself."

"Don't you change your mind over David for I don't want to be the only one thinking him alive."

"I don't plan to just yet. He may have just been delayed." Lady Lucille replied with a tentative smile and got to her feet, "Come, to bed Constance for it has been a long day for both of us."

"Good night Aunt Lucille." Constance placed a kiss on her Lady Lucille's cheek and then left the hall to go to bed.

Chapter 2

December 1146

It was a tall man who walked through the market with his wife on his arm and a ten year old girl's hand in his large one. His blonde hair and beard were beginning to grey. With his just about free hand Pascal pulled his mantle further around him. He looked the image of a Norman knight with a cap over the hair that was just below his ears. His outer tunic, held in by a woven belt, had a look of the Arabic East though the longer inner tunic was plain red. His leather boots had rolled tops which revealed the lining within.

His wife and daughter looked alike with both having brown hair and dark eyes. Both had plaits with ribbon woven into their hair. The main gown reached the ground with a laced bodice. Their girdles round their waists had long tasselled ends hanging down from the bronze hoop that held it all together. His wife's long sleeves hung low meaning she had to hold her arms up so the points did not drag in the mud. Pascal looked round with hazel eyes and snapped at his sixteen year old son,

"Stop dragging your feet. This is a family day out to celebrate Christmastide." Gallien scowled making his father sigh. The youth was more like his mother then himself. Gallien could be demanding and argumentative but there again Pascal had seen that in his own mother, Lady Constance. There had always been moments when his parents had argued passionately however petty the subject. Sometimes, and this bemused him when he was younger, they would suddenly stop mid-sentence. Rarely did he argue at all and he often remained calm receiving strange looks from his mother.

Looking at his son he saw barely any of himself in him. Gallien's hair was pale brown streaked with yellow but his eyes were hazel. He added, "Catch up Gallien."

"Can we have a pie father?" The girl tugged at his arm and Pascal smiled. He looked at his daughter and then at his son again, "Gallien, take your sister and get yourself a meat pie each." He removed his purse from his belt and tipped some coins out of the leather pouch. He held them out and Gallien snatched them up and started out as he called, "Come on then Helene."
His sister removed her hand from Pascal's and ran after her brother and cried out,

"Wait for me."

"You sure she'll be safe with him." The children's mother enquired nervously as she tucked her arm into his. He sighed, "Of course she'll be safe."

"The Holy Lands are once again under threat and we must go save them from the infidels…."
Pascal stopped in his tracks and looked to the man speaking on an upright barrel in the garb of a grubby travelling monk of brown wool. The man went on, "Pope Eugerius has sent out a call to all men for another Crusade to keep the lands of our Lord Jesus Christ safe from the heathens that threaten it. It has been done before and can be done again. Your fathers and grandfathers may have gone and now is your chance to prove yourself worthy of your family's name…"

"You should go Pascal, like your father did." Anne, his wife, said.

"I don't know."

"You always play it safe. It would bring honour to the family all over again. You would be able to say that two generations of Renards have participated in Crusades to preserve the purity of the Holy Lands."

"Ambitious, that's what you are." He remarked to her.

She smiled encouragingly at him and he sighed and gave her a tight smile back. She commented, "Maybe you could go with Gallien while he isn't married."

"I'll think about it." He answered calmly.

"Sometimes I think you are a coward Pascal and not a proper man." She said stiffly. He glared straight ahead and didn't answer his wife; he was no coward, he just liked to think things through first. He turned away from the speaker as he heard a wail behind them. His wife followed suit and took hold of their daughter as she ran to her mother with mud all down her front. Through gulps Helene whined, "He pushed me over and wouldn't give me my pie."

"Gallien!" Pascal said fiercely and glaring; surprising his family for rarely did he get angry.

"She was asking for it." Gallien replied innocently while biting into the untouched pie to claim it as his as well. "Apologise to your sister now."

"Why should I? She's only a girl."

"Gallien, obey your father." Anne replied sternly and with warning while still holding a crying Helene.

"We are going home." Pascal announced calmly and turned away for he was bored of the market and he was feeling so cold he could barely feel his body.

Lady Constance looked to her son as he dropped on to a stool and warmed his hands by the red flames of the central hearth. There was never a time when she did not marvel at how like David he was. It had taken till he was about ten for her to realise that he could quite easily not be Pierre's son.

Even Lady Lucille mentioned it and on her death bed was told the truth. Lady Lucille took it to her grave so Pierre never found out and neither did Sir Henri. As far as Pascal knew his father had once had a brother who never returned from the crusade the pair had gone on in their youth.

Outside it had begun to sleet so the smoke was lingering up in the hall's eaves and rafters. Lady Constance after looking to her son returned to straining her eyes with her sewing though there were three tallow candles around her. Her daughter-inlaw sat beside her and got on with her corner of the tapestry. Helene sat at her mother's feet while Gallien sulkily sat beside his father. Lady Constance enquired when she looked up to rest her eyes, "What's the matter with you all?"

"He needs to grow up." Pascal answered.

"What he needs is something to make him do so like your father and his brother."

Lady Constance remarked sternly before asking, "what was the market like?"

"There was nothing much. There was a speaker calling for men to join a Crusade." Anne remarked with a glance at her husband.

"Is Jerusalem in trouble?" Constance asked

"He didn't say anything like that just that the Holy Lands were in trouble again."

Pascal replied, "I think I should go and take my son with me."

He had now had time about it. He remembered the tales his father used to tell and he realised he wanted to experience it all for himself as well.

Gallien looked on with horror, "I won't go."

"You will obey your father." Anne said sharply.

"You've got to learn to be an adult and a Crusade will make you grow up." Lady

Constance said sternly, "It made your grandfather grow up, may God rest his soul." "Hmpfh." Gallien glowered at his father for having suggested such a thing, "I don't want to go." "What's a Crusade?" Helene piped in and looked to her father.

"It's a war that brings peace to the Holy Lands and protects them for the good Christians of this world." Lady Constance answered her granddaughter and then unsteadily got to her feet, "come with me Pascal. As you have decided to go there are some things you are going to need."

Pascal followed his mother to a small room close to the kitchen, which had been added on to the manor by Sir Henri. She instructed Pascal, "Light the tallow, there should be one in here. There is something you must see."

"I must get a light from the fire."

"Go get it quick then."

Pascal headed out and in a minute returned with a small flame. He lit the tallow and asked, "What do you want me to see?" He looked round and saw the hauberk hung on a rail, his father's. He had looked at it before in his youth wishing he could wear it but in practise he had only worn a padded leather tunic. Now he wondered whether it would fit for his father was slimmer then he. Pascal had always been heavier built then his father and had always assumed it was from his mother who had never lost much of the weight from her pregnancies where only he survived childhood. "If you really want to go then you can't be stopped but take his hauberk. It needs a clean and probably links mended and added to fit you though you never know. Take his sword as well, it's in the chest. It may need a clean and sharpen but otherwise…"

Lady Constance drifted off, "Pascal take Gallien with you as well."

"I know I said I would take him but I think now it would be safer for him to stay. He is the only heir."
Only Helene and Gallien had survived childhood. Others had died in their second or third year of life.
"We have Helene as well."

"But then the family name will be lost."

"You never know." Lady Constance remarked mysteriously. She was wondering if David had survived the last fight for Jerusalem and was living there now but she couldn't be sure at all.

December 1095

The small group of riders, each armed with a hooded hawk perched on their wrist, returned up the muddy track to the white limed wattle and daub manor house with its stone wall for protection. The two men dropped off their horses with the elder of the two looking annoyed as he handed the hawk to a servant that had accompanied them. He pushed brown hair off his face before stalkingg into the house and the hall where his mother sat close to the fire in the centre of the hall with smoke drifting up in wisps to the thatched roof of the place. She sat working on some cloth for a hanging to reduce the drafts of the place.

The manor house was more like a big hall than a house. The stairs were at one end and led up to a large balcony that had the two main bedrooms of the house. Below them and shut off by curtains for the moment were two others, a guest bedroom come private family room. Most of the cooking was done on the central fire of the hall though the oven was out in the courtyard away from the house. Outside, the kennels and stables were lined up against the stone wall perimeter.

She glanced up at her slender tall brown bearded son as he entered in mudsplattered clothes, "I guess there was no luck, but there again is it not the wrong time of year to find much?"

"David is bloody bad luck."

"When will you stop insulting your brother Pierre?" She replied with a gentle sigh,

"you are too harsh on him."

"I do not mind mother." David remarked as he entered in equally mud-splattered clothes. He wore leggings with leather straps wrapped round his calves as well as a short belted blue tunic which worked with his deep blue eyes and his dirty blonde hair framed a masculine square face. He had a clean shaven face with a few cuts from the small sharp knife he used. A cloak covered his shoulders, held on by a large round broach.

Pierre liked to be more fashionable by wearing gowns with the wide sleeved outer ankle length tunic with a cloak held in place with a broach at one shoulder. He also had the fashionable beard and long hair; influenced by the new King, William the
Second. David was clean-shaven. Both were wearing brimless caps. David went on,

"At least he is not hitting me."

"Mmm." Lady Lucille replied.

"I can hit you if you want Davy?" Pierre said to his brother, who was a year and a half younger, with a friendly smile and a wave of his fist.

"Any success?" The final member of the family asked as he arrived in the hall. The two younger men turned as their mother got to her feet revealing the full length of her faded red dress and girdle tied round her waist. Her own blonde hair was hidden, curled up under her wimple that framed her face. Sir Henri Renard was similarly dressed to Pierre though his was decorated with embroidery done by his wife and it was also cleaner. His brown hair was bare to the elements and was looking slightly damp since outside it had begun to rain again.

Sir Henri had smiles all round for his family, "Looking at your face Pierre I am guessing you caught nothing. There is always another day."

"Any news from town Henri?" Lady Lucille enquired.

"Nothing that concerns you wife but you boys maybe interested in what I have to tell you." He replied as he sat down in the single armed high-back chair in the hall. His two sons dropped onto stools with Pierre looking the most eager. David was giving one of the family's old hunting hounds some fuss, the tail gently stirring up the reeds and causing a cloud of dust and crushed herb scents. He didn't look interested but his ears were open as he heard Pierre say, "Do tell us then father."

"The Pope is looking for men to champion our cause and Jesus Christ against the infidels who hold Jerusalem. Interested?"

"Don't know." David remarked with a shrug of his shoulders.

"Pierre?"

"Sounds interesting. It would be better than getting bored around here." Pierre said sounding more enthusiastic than his brother.

"I could try and find some more information out if you want."

"Please."

David got to his feet and left the hall. Pierre watched him go, "he's a coward. All we have learnt goes to waste here. At least with the infidels we can prove we can fight and put it to good use for King, country and God."

"He's less physical than you Pierre." Sir Henri remarked, "he's a thinker. He should have gone to the church. I should send word to our Lord to see if he plans to go." He had never wanted to split the two boys up which was why David, as the younger, had not been directed towards the priesthood. "Would you come father?"

"I think it would be best suited for the new generation of soldiers." Sir Henri answered his son, "someone still needs to look after this manor."

"Mother could." Pierre pointed out. He looked to his mother and saw her smiling. In herself she knew she was capable of looking after the manor but she preferred that her husband did it just to be on the safe side.

"I don't think this Crusade, as it is getting called; would save me from my sins. I have collected too many over the years. This will give you and David the chance to go to Heaven whatever happens, that's what the Pope supposedly said anyway." "What are you doing asking them then Henri?" Lady Lucille commented, "They should both go to safeguard their souls after their deaths. I want them both to go to Heaven." She said firmly as if Pierre was not in the room. "We have lost every other child but I'm not going to lose Pierre and David without knowing whether they go to Heaven or not."

Seeing what was going on Pierre decided to slip out of the hall as quietly as he could due to the rushes on the floor.

Upstairs David was changing his damp leggings though no one was likely to notice whether they were clean or not. Sitting on the window seat looking out of the narrow window with its wooden shutter was a girl from a nearby manor who had lost her whole family to smallpox when she was younger. The Renards had taken her in and though Lady Lucille saw her as a daughter the boys saw her as a best friend who joined in with everything they did. She called Lady Lucille aunt for it had never felt right to call her mother as she could remember her own. Even now she occasionally woke from a nightmare remembering how her real mother had looked on her deathbed.

Her wimple lay in her lap and her loose brown hair hung down her back. Constance, though dressed as a woman was more of a tomboy thanks to living with the brothers since she was six years old. Her feminine face didn't however reveal such a nature although she had a well built body from all the riding and climbing she had down with the boys. Her figure was prefect for child bearing though she had not a thought for children or even marriage and her aunt and uncle hadn't brought it up recently.

She moaned to David, "I hate having my hair all hidden away and a wimple is so hot. I shouldn't even be wearing as I'm not married."

"You've got to remember that there are many your age who are married and no husband wants their pretty young wife running off with another man."

"Still, why does Aunt Lucille make me wear it?"   "So that you don't go off with the first handsome man who makes your heart flutter because he says pretty words to you. There are plans for you I'm sure." David answered calmly since he was use to her moaning.

"Is she moaning again?" Pierre asked with a smile as he entered the room he shared with his brother.

"Her life just isn't exciting enough." David commented with a teasing smile.

"All you women do is moan." Pierre added.

"That's uncalled for. I could be marrying one of you and I could easily make your life a living Hell." She pointed out. Ever since she had become of a marriageable age rumours floating around that she, now at sixteen, was to marry one of the brothers though neither at twenty-two knew which one it would be. Between the three of them it had in fact become a bit of a joke.

"I think we would have married by now if it really was going to happen Connie." Pierre pointed out.

"Who said it would be you Long-shanks?" She remarked back. Pierre had gained the nickname from his brother when he had been very much the taller of the two before David had caught up with him.

"I am the elder and will inherit the manor and need an heir." Pierre pointed out stiffly, "Davy here has to go and find himself some rich heiress or a lord who will take him on and pay him to be in his guard and don't call me that."
"What if I like him better?"

"Don't get me involved in this please." David interrupted as he finished changing his clothes, "You'd best get that wimple back on before mother catches you without it otherwise she might begin to think that you are easy with us two."
"You have a dirty mind Davy." She exclaimed.

"He is a man Connie, like me. Such thoughts could be making up for the fact he is not interested in war." Pierre said.

"I wish I was a man." Constance sighed and turned her head to look down on the manor's garden out of hazel eyes. "No you don't. You have it easy, staying at home all the time." David pointed out. "You don't have to give birth." She exclaimed, "at least as a man you can go out and have some excitement. You think I haven't heard but I have. The Pope is after men to go and rescue Jerusalem from the heathens who call themselves Mohammeds. Now how is it that you get to go off to far off lands?."

"Are you mad?" David exclaimed, "It means death for all."

"And Heaven." Pierre added, "Mother wants us both to go Davy. She wants our souls saved before we turn them black." David sighed for if their parents wanted them to go then he couldn't make any objections, "It was pointless asking our opinions then wasn't it?"

"I think if we were both completely off the idea then they wouldn't force us." "I can blame this on you then Longshanks." David said in annoyance. Before he could hear any more on how his parents wanted them to go to the Holy Lands he left their bedroom, which was beginning to feel crowded. Constance looked annoyed as her cousin left and at Pierre she asked, "Do you do it on purpose?"

"He's just weak. He's not made to be a soldier so I don't know why father got him trained as one. He should have sent him to the church."

"You are horrible to him." Constance said angrily and got to her feet, "and he's your brother."

"That's what makes you a girl." Pierre responded with a sneer and mimicked her feminine voice, "Horrible." She stamped her foot in anger and then ran from the room leaving him smiling to himself and feeling proud of the mimic of his mother's ward.

She found David by the kennels stroking one of the hounds who was also eagerly licking the young man's hand. She looked down at him sitting on the bench. She said, "I'm sorry about Pierre."

"You shouldn't be since he is my brother. I should be the one apologising." He looked up at her.

"He's a rotter though."

"That's because he is my brother." David remarked as he returned to the hound at his feet.

"But he insults you Davy."

"I'm use to it. Why are you so concerned for me anyway?"

She shrugged her shoulders. He frowned and asked with fear, "Don't tell me that you are attracted to me?"

"I am not attracted to you." She answered fiercely, "or Long-shanks at that. If you aren't going to be nice to me either I'll leave you to your dogs." She turned and stomped away. David raised his eyebrows in astonishment and wondered what had got into Constance and in the end decided it was her time of the month. He looked to the dog and sighed. He felt sure that she wasn't admitting something. Whatever it was she probably wouldn't be allowed to marry him. It was more likely to be Pierre since he was the elder.

At dinner that evening a silent seemed to hang over the family. Constance, who was normally the most talkative, was quiet only because she was still annoyed with the brothers. Pierre was eating as heartily as ever but David wasn't. David was mulling over what his father had told them about the planned Crusade. He wasn't sure whether he could go out and kill others though he had learnt to do so and was a very capable soldier. He was picking at his food as he thought it all over. Lady Lucille watched her son with concern, "Are you well Davy?"

"Don't ask such silly questions Lucille. Of course he's fine and use his proper name.

He is not a child anymore; he is a man and remember that. You should know better."

Sir Henri remarked sternly, "And David stop picking at that food. Eat it properly like Pierre is. What are you thinking about anyway? I can see you thinking so don't say you aren't."

"Nothing much."

"I've seen you like this before. Have you and Pierre had another argument?" Sir Henri demanded.

"No." Pierre said looking up, "It's the Crusade the Pope wants us to go on. He's a coward, he doesn't want to go."
"That's not true." David answered defensively.

"Boys, please." Their mother said fiercely, "If you must argue do it quietly." "I'm not a coward. It's just that if we both went, what if we both died?" He looked at his father who was now looking thoughtful and added, "Who would inherit the manor then?"

"You are right but doing the family name proud is more important so you are both to go. You are both sensible and I'm sure you'll come back alive with many stories to tell. You'll also both go to Heaven once you have helped rescue Jerusalem from those infidels." Sir Henri said fiercely, "I am having no more excuses understand or I will send you into the church."
David bowed his head, "Yes father."

David threw in his playing cards early only because he couldn't concentrate on the game. Constance followed him a few minutes later. Lady Lucille frowned at her husband, "There's something going on in David's mind. You should talk to him about this."

"You need to talk to Constance as well. She's still boyish." Sir Henri returned stiffly and threw his cards in, "The idea of the boys going off wasn't meant to turn this family into a mess. I've got… Go to bed Pierre, this is private." He turned to his son. Pierre bowed his head and stood. He gave his mother a kiss on the cheek before heading up the stairs to his shared bedroom. On their own Sir Henri returned to looking at his wife, "I've got one son who doesn't seem to want to go, another who is eager to and your ward who needs to calm down and understand that she is a woman and not a man. I can't believe this; my family is falling apart." He replied as he led them both up the stairs.

"This Crusade thing came all of a sudden Henri, no wonder everyone appears to be fragmenting. Its not like out sons have ever travelled further then your brother's."

"I don't understand you wife." He remarked as he held the door open for he. As she entered she asked, "What do you mean?"

"Earlier today you wanted them to go to save their souls but now I'm getting the impression you'd rather keep them safely tucked away from the rest of the world here. Make up your mind."

"Let me tell you something then. I'm a mother. I brought them into this world and brought them up to be two good lads. I want them to go and bring honour to this family but also there is the fear of losing them both in rapid succession. I wouldn't want to lose both my babies in one fell swoop." She said in her defence.

He smiled at her as he helped her out of her clothes, "You, my dear, are unbelievable sometimes."

She smiled, "Thank you. You must talk to David though, make him see sense that this is wise."

"You want him to go then? I know he's your favourite and only because he follows you in his nature."

"He's not going to inherit this land and needs some money which he could earn on the Crusade. He could gain a reputation which means he would find it easier to find a wife when he returns since Constance and Pierre are to marry."

"When did we decide that marriage?" He looked at her, turning his head from where he had been staring up at the canopy of their bed.

"I think it should happen." She answered and moved closer to her husband, "We need the next generation to begin appearing and she is growing older. If we wait too long she will be unable to bear us any grandchildren and that will be the end of the family name living here before it's barely settled in. Anyhow, aren't you meant to be the one concerned about the future of your family name since I only married into this family."

"You are a wise woman my dear." He smiled and kissed her lovingly. She put an arm across him and moved closer to him.

Whereas they were obviously going to sleep the three young people weren't. They were all in the boys' dimly lit room where there were only two tallow candles lit and the moonlight that was sneaking in between the wooden shutter and the wall. A breeze caused the tallow flames to flicker and the shutter to creek. Pierre was having a go at David who was sitting on his bed next to a cross-legged Constance, "You could easily have ruined it for us to go to the Holy Lands. Father could have changed his mind because of you."

"It's not his fault." Constance put in.

"I don't need you defending me Connie." David snapped. He stood up and looked to his brother, "You might want to go but I don't."

"I don't want to go alone Davy." Pierre said in slight fear, "We've always done everything together, don't let this split us."

"I want to come with you too." Constance demanded.

The two young men ignored her as Pierre said, "Father is going to speak with you on it. You will have put worries in his head because of you. Why don't you want to go Davy? Think of the honour, helping Christendom against the infidels." "I don't want to talk about it." David answered as he crossed to the window and firmly shut the shutter. "I want to come with you." Constance repeated in annoyance.

"No!" The brothers said at her fiercely.

"I'll come with you Pierre if Davy won't." She offered as she persisted.

"David?" Pierre looked to his brother.

"All right, but only to stop Connie from making a fool of herself." David sighed reluctantly. Pierre smiled with glee while Constance looking like a black cloud was looming above her head. However, whatever happened, she planned to go with them but she just had to come up with an idea that would work. Pierre said to David, "You must tell father then."

"Tomorrow then. Now can I go to bed? Are you coming Long-shanks or will you be waking me up later?"   "I'm coming."

"See you tomorrow then boys." Constance gave the two young men a kiss on the cheek each before leaving the room and creeping through her uncle and aunt's bedroom and then down the stairs to the bedroom off the hall, which she shared with the two household maids when one or the other wasn't messing around with Pierre.   David removed everything but his shirt before getting into the bed he shared with Pierre while both were single. It wasn't always the best experience especially when Pierre decided to take over the bed but he was use to it. There was a heavy sigh from Pierre as he slipped in but David decided not to ask what the problem was. He turned his back on his older brother and hugged his feather filled pillow as he closed his eyes. For a brief moment he opened them again and with fingers searched for the feather that was sticking up through the fabric and pulled it out as he found it and then settled back down again.

Chapter 3

May 1147

The whole family was on the dockside of Dartmouth to see father and son off. Around them was chaos as boats were loaded up with supplies for the men on both the English and Flemish boats. Sailors were pulling on ropes and unfurling the large rectangular sails for final checks. Families of the departing men crowded the dock saying farewell to fathers, brothers, sons and sweethearts with some being more emotional than others. It was mainly men going this time round though there were a few widows who would be cooking and cleaning clothes for the soldiers and knights. Lady Constance was with Pascal and she appeared to be placing a motherly kiss on his cheek but instead she said, "I want a word with you in private."

"What about?"

"Just come with me." She drew him away from his family and gave him a tight smile for how he was dressed now, in the chain mail tunic, which made her think of David, "You look good in that hauberk."

"What do you want to talk about?"

Lady Constance looked round and saw her grandchildren staring up at the flapping sails before the sailors got them under control in the strong sea breeze. Looking back to her son she said, "There is something you need to know about yourself."

He frowned, "I don't understand."

"Please, take this letter. Whatever you do, don't open it. If you reach Jerusalem and find a man called David Renard…"

"My uncle? I thought he was dead." Pascal interrupted feeling confused as he had always been told that his uncle David had died in the Crusade.

"He may not be…" Constance hesitated then. Both hers and Pascal's hands were on the thick parchment. She wondered if she could trust him but there again she had always been able to trust David, "give this to him if he lives. If he doesn't burn it.
Promise me you will never ever open it."

"I… mother what is this all about?"

"Have I your word?" She demanded
"Of course you have."

"Good." It was only then that Constance let go of the letter and as he slipped it into his leather pouch at his belt she added, "when you have a chance put it somewhere safer. Always keep it close."
"Yes mother but how will I recognise if it is him?"

"I feel you will know it is him. Now go and may God be on your side and try not to be shocked when you meet your uncle."
"You speak as if you know he lives."

Lady Constance smiled, "I can't assume any other way. Go say farewell to your…" The tears began to fall then. She had lost David to the Crusade, half her husband to it and there was still the chance she might lose her son and grandson, "… to your family. Look, they are waiting."

As the ships left the land behind them Pascal and Gallien leant on the side. Above them the square sail was unfurled to catch the wind to take them down through the Bay of Biscay and the west coast of Iberia before going on through the straits and across the Mediterranean to hopefully reach the Holy Lands. Orders were shouted up to the man at the tiller who constantly adjusted the large long boat through the waves. As they bulldozed and bounced in turn through the waves Gallien swallowed to hold down the bile rising in his throat. His stomach was tumbling over and over. His father appeared not to have noticed.

Pascal was lost in his thoughts as he contemplated what his mother had said to him. He was bewildered by his mother's words. He was wondering what his uncle would look like and whether he was anything like his father considering they were brothers and the priest had spoken of the special connections God granted such men. For a moment he wanted to skip the Crusade and go straight to Jerusalem to find the mysterious uncle. He fingered the letter in his money pouch and for a moment considered breaking the seals and opening it. He looked to the skies for guidance and accepted that it would be too sinful for this trip to break the promise he had made to his mother.

He only took notice of Gallien as his son brought up his breakfast. He saw that Gallien was looking a little green round the edges of his face. He took hold of his son and remarked, "You'd best come away from the side and sit down."

"How long will we be at sea father?"

"I'm sure you'll get over it soon." Pascal attempted to console his son as he sat him down in front of a cage of chickens and a few sheep. Looking at the animals he commented, "I wonder how many of these will die before we eat them."

"I don't care." Gallien said feeling self pity for himself from being sea sick. He also felt jealous of the fact his father did not appear bothered by the sea which was playing turmoil with his stomach. Pascal smiled in amusement at his son's remarked as he sat down beside him.

September 1096

It was all arranged and though Lady Lucille wished that her ward did not go with her two sons to Normandy she couldn't stop it. Constance wanted to see the brothers off from Normandy, when they would truly be going off on the Crusade as soldiers with Duke Robert Curthose of Normandy. She hoped to also get the chance to join them; dressed up and pretending she was a man like them. The man they were to stay with was Sir Henri's brother and since he was unlikely to take much notice of Constance she hoped to join the two men on the Crusade. She did have slight misgivings when they crossed the English Channel since she felt seasick. Neither of the two men took much notice, as they were more concerned about their horses for without them they felt they couldn't really be called knights.

The group of three men and one woman and a packhorse rode up to the Norman manor house that was similar to their home in England though it was made of stone with a high wall and moat around it. Unlike England Normandy had been turbulent with plenty of fighting within the state's boundaries. David and Pierre dressed in their chain mail armour so they could become use to the weight. As well as the chain mail knee length harbeck there were leather leggings and gauntlets. When it had been first put on over leather padding their shoulders were weighed down especially with the chain mail hood down. Their horses could cope with the weight of man dressed in chain mail since they were almost as large and strong as carthorses.

Their helmets hung down from their saddlebags along with their kite shaped body length shields, which were painted red. Their double-edged swords hung down from their waists knocking against their legs. They held unadorned lances in their hands with Owen carrying spare shafts.

The young men's uncle was there to greet them with a grin for all of them. He hugged and kissed the cheeks of his nephews once they had slipped off their horses, "To think that my big brother created two strapping men like you. And who is this pretty lady?"

Like his nephews he hugged and gave Constance a kiss on each cheek. David introduced her, "This is our mother's ward, Constance Berkeley."

"You are therefore welcome as well Constance." He smiled warmly at her, "I am guessing you came all this way just to make sure that they got here safely."

Constance blushed, "You could put it that way."

"You'll make a good wife my dear, worrying for them. You'll have to just hope they both return safe and alive."

"Of course we will, we have God on our side." Pierre said with confidence. David glanced at his brother for he felt that there had been too much force in his confidence as if he didn't believe it. He said nothing then but caught up with Pierre as soon as he could.

For once in his life Pierre looked on the pale side when David found him wandering in the garden. David put an arm on his brother as he remarked with a teasing smile, "Don't tell me you are having second thoughts Long-shanks?" "I'm not." Pierre answered defensively. "Come on, you can't really be that confident we have God on our side." "Don't say such things otherwise you might spook the whole Crusade. If people didn't believe then it might fail. With faith in God we will be able to beat those Mohammeds and rescue the city of our Lord from them. We will do it because we have God on our side." Pierre answered with determination and confidence and this time there was no evidence of misgiving, "We have got this far and father has put money into this so we can't turn back. We are doing this

for the honour it will bring our family, remember that Davy."
He looked sternly at his younger brother. David blinked and
said nothing, waiting for Pierre to go on for he was sure there
was more to be said. Pierre finally admitted, "I feel a little
afraid, yes. I've admitted it, happy now or do you think I
should confess? Come on you are feeling afraid as well since
you were the one to have the misgivings first. This is the first
time we have truly been away from home Davy so we are
both allowed to have some fear of what is to come. This is
our first proper test of skill as soldiers and I can only hope
that we are good enough to survive. I know we will go to
Heaven but I'd rather I lived; I don't know about you."
David nodded, "I'd prefer to live as well."

"Glad to hear it." Pierre looked relieved, "Can we make a
pact?"

"What sort of one?"

"We'll both live through this to see another day, a peaceful
one. Agreed?" He held out his hand.

"Agreed." David gave his brother a tight smile and shook
the hand that was held out. Pierre smiled, "We'll make it
together brother and bring much honour to the family name
of Renard."

"Are you two gossiping old women going to come in for
dinner or not?" Sir Raoul

Renard called over, "I don't know why I'm the one
looking for you though?"   "We are coming uncle." David
called back and began to head towards the older bearded
man.

"We are waiting for you. What were you talking about
anyway?"

"Things." David replied and glanced back at his brother.
Pierre's eyes narrowed at him, warning him not to say a word

about their pact. He thought it best to be kept a secret otherwise it would appear that neither had confidence in God. He gave his uncle a tight smile as the man turned and headed back to the house.

Over dinner there was the general banter of catching up on old and new news since several large miles of water separated the Norman family. Sir Henri Renard had been a late arrival in England, after the invasion by William the Conqueror in 1066, five years before Pierre had been born and he had married an Anglo-Saxon woman.
Sir Raoul asked, "So my brother is well then?"

"As well as can be expected." Pierre answered as he drank more ale from his cup. "We'll head off in a day or two to join the Duke, that's if it doesn't decide to pour with rain."
"I feel it's going to rain Raoul. My joints are causing me pain again." Lady Marie, the man's wife, put in. Her joints grew sore and swollen in the damp due to they being arthritic, especially her knees.

"We'll just have to brave it I suppose if the rains not too heavy, agreed?" Sir Raoul looked to his nephews, "you both need to be knighted then you'll get more rewards and respect." His uncle remarked, "Perhaps we can get Duke Robert to do it. You realise we are going to be one of the few in this army. Most are from Flanders under the Count there."
"Father should have just sent him to a Monastery." Pierre interrupted, "He's not made of the right stuff to be a soldier."
"He just needs a chance to bring all he has learnt together."

"Are you going as well sir?" Constance asked with sudden fear. If Sir Raoul was to be going then she may not be able to get away with going with her cousins. She had got this far but she didn't know how much further she would be able to get.
"Of course I am, as far as the army to make sure they get there safely. I promised my brother that much." Sir Raoul smiled.

"Can I join you?"

"If you really want to." Sir Raoul looked slightly shocked that the young woman wanted to ride with them on a journey that would be on the boring side if he was honest with himself.

Constance slipped into the men's bedroom. She shook David awake though he tried to brush her away at first. Finally he opened his eyes, "What is it you want Connie?"

"Can I speak with you in private?"

With a sigh he got up and followed her out of the room. Down in the hall they sat close to the dying fire. He yawned as he moaned, "What is this about since I'm tired? We are going hunting tomorrow remember."

"I know I can trust you Davy. I want to come with you."

"We've both told you that you can't Connie. Stop asking us."

"Perhaps I should rephrase it then. I am coming with you David." She said sternly and using his proper name to show she really meant it.

"How?" He asked.

"I'm cutting my hair and going to act as your servant."

"Mine?"

"You won't give me away. I know I can trust you with a secret."

He sighed but warned, "You can only blame yourself if you are caught or you discover its not all you think it is. This is a man's world you are entering now and its dangerous, cruel and rough. There won't be any comforts once we reach the Holy

Lands or while we are travelling."

"I don't care."

"You won't be able to carry out this pretence, you're a woman remember." "Stop telling me that." She snapped and then calming went on, "I don't want to be at home worrying and waiting for the both of you to return or maybe not at all." "Don't say that. How am I going to make everyone believe that you are my servant though? We only need one between the pair of us and I'm not even an official knight so don't deserve one. There is also the fact that Uncle Raoul is coming with us and he will be expecting you to return with him." David calmly pointed out all the errors in her plan but she didn't let him get her downhearted. She remained as determined as ever to go with the young men. With annoyance she said, "Fine then; if I'm unsuccessful I'll be the good girl you want me to be but if I do this you aren't to tell anyone, not even Pierre."

"You trust me to? What if Long-shanks finds out? He's not stupid you know." "If he finds out he finds out." She shrugged her shoulders.

"Why do you trust me at all?" David asked out of curiosity.

She looked at the dying fire and then at her cousin, "I just do. You've never told tales on me when I was doing things..." "Like climbing trees to get that Peregrine back." He smiled at her making her smile back and comment, "You encouraged me to."

"Long-shanks wouldn't get it and I had that broken wrist. If you've said enough can I go back to bed?" He yawned and wiped at his tired eyes.

"You promise not to tell?"

"I promise." He sighed as he got to his feet, "It will be a shame to lose all that hair mind you." He looked into her face and she gave him a tight smile as she replied, "It has to be done."

Lady Marie kissed each young man on the cheek though for Sir Raoul she kissed his lips. With her nephews she pressed a small wooden box each into their hands. Both looked at the simply carved box in wonder before she explained, "I hope that will be enough for the whole time. It's an ointment for when you get bruised. I know how sore you can get from fighting. I have seen my son practicing with his father and he can be harsh with his attacks. Both of you are to take care and return safely here you understand. I will want to hear about what happens."

"Of course we will return here on our way home once we have taken Jerusalem from the heathens." Pierre replied with a smile for his aunt.

"Good." She smiled, "Good luck and bring honour to the family."

"We will do that." David promised, "We don't plan to disgrace either you and uncle or our father." He kissed his aunt on the cheek before climbing on to his horse. His brother and uncle got on to theirs while a servant helped Constance up. Lady Marie looked to her husband, "You behave yourself Raoul, don't drink too much or get into a fight."

"I don't plan to." He growled from his saddle as he adjusted his cloak around his thickly set body. He was only wearing it since his wife had promised rain and casting his eyes to the sky he saw that black clouds were forming in the distance. If it caught up with them they would be in trouble, as the rain would rust the young men's chain mail since they weren't wearing their plain white surcoats. Rain had been a long time in coming however and it was needed for the manor's garden and fields.

"Watch for the rain."

"We need it in the fields. Let's hope your joints are right."

"They are always right. You should get going before the rain reaches us. I will see you in a few days." She gave him a small loving smile. She realised that when she first married him she had hated him. Now with so much time spent with him and the discovery that he was quite a caring man; even if forgetful at times and prone to fits of daydreaming, she loved him except when he had drunk too much.

"You take care of yourself." He smiled at her before spurring his horse forward to lead the way out of his manor and east towards Flanders.

Chapter 4

Late September 1096

Arriving at Count Robert of Flanders' homeland they saw a camp of tents and tethered horses spreading out around the motte and bailey castle. They had to halt their horses but only because they didn't know where they should go now that they had arrived. Out loud Sir Raoul remarked, "I suppose we should go and find His Grace to let him know he has some supporters. He doesn't have many on this side of the water though what he'll say about you coming from his brother I don't know."

"The King didn't send us here. We came because we wanted to." Pierre corrected his uncle sternly; "The English are all cowards if they have no Norman blood in them. We should find someone to take us to the Duke." He spurred his horse forward and began to head through the camp before either his brother or uncle could stop him. They hurried after him and hoped no one would get angry with them riding on horseback since others were leading their horses by the reins. If the way had been narrow perhaps Pierre would have got off but as it seemed to be the main thoroughfare up to the gates of the castle he didn't try to show any politeness.

Reaching the gates with the others not far behind Pierre slipped off and demanded,

"Let the Duke know we have arrived."

"And who are you to give orders?" The soldier on duty retorted straight back. Sir Raoul got down off his horse and with more courtesy asked, "Is it possible to get an audience with His Grace, the Duke of Normandy?"

"Who should I say it is?"

"Sir Raoul Renard de Verneuesses with his two nephews who wish to join his army. They represent the better half of Norman society who have choosen to join him on his fight for the recovery of the Holy Lands from the infidels."

"Save your speech for the Duke." The infantryman sneered but let them through. Word appeared to travel quickly through the castle as they were welcomed into the castle's hall even if it wasn't to stay for dinner. The Duke gave them a smile as the three men bowed and Constance curtseyed. He remarked, "I am glad to find I have some support for this Crusade among my knights."

"My nephews come from my brother in England sir."

"And they are with me because my own brother does not care for the rescue of the

Holy Land and Jerusalem. I am glad to welcome you then. Is it just you two?"

"Yes Your Grace."

"So you aren't to come Knight?" The Duke looked to Sir Raoul.

"My apologies sir but if I was younger I would have joined but my wife expects me back and I do not have the youth and strength to be gallivanting to the Holy Lands. Though I'm not with you I support you, Your Grace, in my prayers. My nephews will make your army something to be proud of. They will bring honour to your name as well as our own. They are both good men and well trained sodliers and will do all they can to rescue Jerusalem from the heathen Muslims."

"Are they knights?" The Duke asked. His eyes remained on the older man though they briefly flickered to the younger men who stood either side of their uncle.

"Not as yet. Neither have seen battle to earn the priviledge." Robert Curthose, as he had been nicknamed, looked thoughtful for a moment before getting to his feet, "they need to be knight then. Step forward."
Sir Raoul nudged his nephews forward. David obligingly stepped forward and bowed his head, "Your Grace." Pierre stood straight with pride.

The Duke approached and studied the two young men as he asked, "you are both trained? Do you want to be knights? There are so few men from my Duchy then perhaps it would look good to have only knights fighting apart from the archers and infantry. Have only knighted cavalrymen, what do you think?" He looked at David questioningly as he passed the younger brother.

"I do not lead any men into battle sir but people would look with honour in their eyes if they were to know you have only the best knights, each deserving their title Your Grace." David replied calmly though inside he was afraid that he may have said the wrong thing. Robert Curthose smiled as he commented, "My dear younger brother will be jealous to know I have you with me."

"Thank you sir."

"We'll make you both knights and make your parents proud." The Duke stepped forward and David and Pierre knelt before him. They bowed their heads and received the blow to the back of their necks from the Duke's hand making them titled knights and not just horsemen, "I announce you as knights and so from now on you are Sir David Renard and Sir Pierre Renard. So I now have two English Knights in my midst. You are lucky to have arrived today for we leave tomorrow. David, you must join me at my table tonight." David glanced behind at his brother and cousin wondering why he had been picked out. Everything had gone too far too fast and he had never planned it to happen. He hoped his brother wouldn't get angry for this occurring to him instead of Pierre. He looked pleadingly at Pierre who shrugged his shoulders as if to say 'it happens'. Looking at his uncle and Constance they both were smiling, pleased for him. Looking back at the Duke he asked, "May my brother join me?"

"At least some have consideration for their brothers." The Duke remarked with a sneer, addressing it his absent younger brother, William, King of England. He was the brother he hated because he owned more land and prestige then the Duchy of Normandy did. Finally he smiled, "He is welcomed as well. Tonight the pair of you can sleep on the floor in here. It will be foolish to put up a tent."

"Thank you Your Grace." David answered hurriedly before Pierre could object for he felt sure that his brother would. "At least you two are brothers who can be together comfortably. I hope what you have remains so."

Everyone was up when the two brothers finally woke up in the morning. Seeing the bustle about the place they quickly got up along with their uncle. None of them noticed whether Constance was around. So as not to be in the way Sir Raoul decided to leave. With so much going on he had vanished into one of his daydreams of the past and the skirmishes he had fought in and completely forgot that he was meant to be returning with Constance. It was only when he reached home and was reprimanded by his wife that he remembered and it was too late. He wasn't sure how he would tell his brother of his ward's absence.

The two brothers accompanied their uncle out of the keep and then both embraced the older man before his horse appeared and he climbed up on to it. They waved him off and then as he rode out began to walk down and across the drawbridge to watch the madness of the camp falling to pieces as each tent was allowed to fall in on itself and then were loaded on to mules or carts. The other knights had servants to do the hard labour while the infantry and archers did the work themselves. The brothers had one servant to share between them but that was one of the few things they had agreed to share on the Crusade. David was the first to turn away as he remarked, "It will be a while yet." "I'm going to continue watching; this is quite enjoyable. There was a mule that bucked back there, and they hadn't even tied its load down." Pierre smiled at his brother and David did as well as he returned, "That was quite funny. I might return but I'm hungry. Do you want anything?" "If you can find anything." Pierre answered but already he was turning back to watch the decamping chaos.

Back inside David wandered about in search of food and wasn't expected it to be handed to him. His eyes narrowed as he tried to workout where he had seen the face before with the smiling hazel eyes of success and the smiling red round lips of pride. It clicked then in him, the face was too feminine. Cautiously, as he took the stale bread from her, he asked, "Connie?"
She smiled even more, "You recognised me. Don't tell Longshanks remember."

"What should I call you now then? Why did you have to cut your hair? It was so nice and long." "You liked it?" She asked becoming uncertain for a moment.

"You looked nice with it long." He gave her a shy smile, "How am I going to explain you away Connie?"
"Call me Constant, that should make your life easy. I don't know how you are going to explain me."
"Where did you get your clothes Con..., Constant?"

"Yours fit me." She admitted with a teasing smile though she had had to do some late night sewing to actually make them fit better as he was wider than her. He eyed her but found himself smiling as well. He put an arm round her, "Come on you." She twisted away from him, "You'd best not do that since I look like a man now. You are going to have to be careful from now on…" She looked thoughtful and then added, "… I've got it. You found me and took pity on me; that is like you to do that sort of thing."

"Err.." Now looking at her David was no longer sure of her plan working, "that wouldn't work."

"You can't back out now. Your uncle has gone and I would need an escort for the sake of my safety to get back." Constance protested.

"Perhaps you should join the wagons. I think it would work out better if you stayed out of the way unless necessary. Pierre isn't going to fall for your attempts to not pretend to be you. You've lived with us too long for us not to recognise you from the way you do things."

Constance pouted and sulkily submitted as she realised David was right and she hadn't quite thought her plan through, "alright. Don't think I won't come find you though. You can't hide from me."

"Cheer up now. You are off on the adventure you wanted now though only the Lord knows how mother and father are going to react when they realise you are with us."

"Hmpfh." She crossed her arms and turned away from him. With a shrug of his shoulders David abandoned his cousin to her lot. She wasn't meant to have come and she had done this of her own free will. He would help her only if she got herself into a really sticky situation.

David returned to Pierre with the bread Constance had given him. He was to be found still watching the decamping of the army under the command of the two Roberts who were cousins, Robert Curthose of Normandy and Count Robert of Flanders. David stepped up to his brother's side and handed yesterday's bread over,

"Eat that. Anything of interest occurred?"

"Nah but I think we are nearly ready to leave."

"I'm glad we didn't have to put our tent up for the taking down of it." "So am I though tonight we may have to. It hasn't rained yet." Pierre looked skywards and then to his brother and went on with a mouth full of bread, "It could easily rain soon."
"That is true. Are our horses ready?"

"They should be." Pierre turned to look into the dirt courtyard and then noticed

Constance. He nudged David who turned, "Who's that David?"

"Owen must have dragged him out of the mud somewhere to help." David lied and almost instantly wished he didn't have to lie as well as wishing he hadn't promised his female cousin.
"Well we don't need him. What did Owen think he was doing suggesting there was work for him?" At the woman dressed as a man he shouted, "Scat! Get lost!" "Leave it Pierre." David put a hand on his brother, "He will be useful for the moment."
"I suppose so." Pierre didn't look happy but still he agreed. To Constance he said,

"You won't get any pay from us."

"Fine… I only want to serve." Constance's voice came out to feminine and rapidly she deepened her voice the best she could and hoped it would fool Pierre. Pierre seemed fooled for the time being since he turned back on her, "Go find Owen then." Constance turned and headed off to do as Pierre told.

        Into the silence that had been left Pierre remarked, "He looked familiar somehow."

David froze in fear that his older brother had recognised Constance for who she was. Pierre went on without even glancing at his brother, "I can't put my finger on it but never mind. I'm probably imagining it."

"I'm sure you are." David answered stiffly and looked to his brother. There was nothing on Pierre's face to suggest that he was playing with David; no twitching smile that Pierre used when he was winding his younger brother up. David froze again when Pierre commented, "I'm glad Connie isn't with us. Only the Lord knows what would have happened if we had given into her. She'll get back home safely I'm sure." David stared at his older brother amazed that all the excitement of decamping and setting out on the crusade had completely erased from Pierre's head the fact that Constance had travelled to the camp with them and that their uncle had headed home on his own. His mouth almost hung open with amazement. Before he could say anything that would give Constance away the Norman Duke appeared with a smile for them both. He put a hand on each shoulder; "We'll be off shortly my dear Englishmen if I can call you fellows that."

"If that is what you wish Your Grace." David said before Pierre could say anything.

"Looking forward to the journey?"

"I think it's going to rain." Pierre informed the Duke.

"Pierre." David hissed feeling embarrassed by his brother's comment. The Duke hadn't noticed since he had wandered off.

"In favour already." Pierre sneered.

"I didn't expect it to happen." David answered in defence, "I didn't want it to happen Long-shanks, honest. I would have been happy for you so please be happy for me."

"Come on, some are getting in their saddles." Pierre replied without making any comment on what David had said. He didn't like the fact that the Duke was interested in David and not him. At least the Duke had acknowledged them both. For a second, before he shook the thought away, he feared that the Duke may be trying to make David the friendly brother he didn't have and David was his supportive brother and no one else's. As if to reassure himself he turned to David, "You wouldn't leave me would you?"

"What's got into you?" David turned and looked with confusion to his brother, "why would I leave you? We've created so many pacts that we are unlikely to ever be apart."

"Sssh." He hissed with warning, "No one needs to know about them." He glared at David who felt himself shrinking back from him. Pierre turned and feeling angry heaved himself up on to his horse.

They began close to the front at the invitation from the Duke but gradually they fell back to the middle of the leisurely moving column of men. The supplies were all to the back of a large selection of carts and mules along with the hired washerwomen and camp followers though for the moment they were few and mainly servants. The long continuous stream of soldiers on foot and horseback with banners flying in the wind marched southwards with little foreboding of what was to come. They moved with much noise down the roads of the countryside with jangling horse reins, chatter, laughter and sporadic singing. It looked like a motley band of men more than an army what with the noise and banners. It was more like a crowd of rowdy cheerful pilgrims with high expectations of what was to come then an army of disciplined soldiers going to their possible deaths. From above they looked like a giant silvery snake glittering in the sunlight before the rain, slowly slipping through the landscape.

Seeing how many there were both brothers began to realise that they were only a tiny part of the army heading to the Holy Lands especially when many others had already set off the month before. There appeared to be no hurry for the mass of armoured men to go anywhere fast. No one seemed to be looking that far into the future. To some of the younger men it was an adventure. They were all probably hiding their fear of death well behind the belief they would go to Heaven and faith that God was on their side David considered. To his brother Pierre remarked, more friendly now as if he had had a chance to calm down and needed it, "We are finally going and there's no turning back now. Neither one of us are going to die because we have God on our side."

David nodded solemnly but didn't really appear to be listening since he was turning his head to look behind him. Pierre looked behind as he asked, "What are you trying to see?"

"Nothing." David hurriedly answered, too fast since his brother demanded, "What are you hiding from me?"

"Nothing." He had promised Constance so he wasn't going to tell. He was trying to find her in the column even though he had told her to stay well back. He hoped she wouldn't be looking out of place as bewildered as he was. Never had he been in such a large group of people; even market day wasn't as bad as this mess of people.   "David?"

"There is nothing I'm hiding from you."

"Why do you keep looking behind then?"

"There is just so many people and I don't want to find us right at the back with the supplies." David lied to get his brother off his back.

"We won't find ourselves there." Pierre answered confidently and then left David to his nervous glances.

Chapter 5

July 1097

The Crusaders had laid siege to Nicaea, a walled city near Constantinople. To the west was a lake which came right up to the walls. The rest of the city was surrounded by high walls with towers scattered along each length. On behalf of their allies the Crusaders attacked and entered the city only to their dismay to lose any chance of plundering the city as the Byzantines claimed the victory theirs. The Saracen leader, Kilij Arslan, was not pleased that the city had fallen so easily and planned revenge.

Having left Nicaea to their celebrating allies the Crusaders headed south as two separate groups, coming to the town of Dorylaeum. Hearing that the Christians were on their way Kilij Arslan set himself and his army up on the hillsides around the town to wait for the Crusaders to appear over the hills. With them sighted he allowed them to set up camp close to the riverbank. He gave an order to the scouts, "Watch over them. Any suspicious activities then let me know." He planned to attack them when they were at their weakest; early in the morning when they wouldn't suspect anything and that was only because the Crusaders didn't know of their enemy's presence near by. The Crusaders weren't aware of the enemy camped so near. They had their own concerns with their allies, whether they were untrustworthy and planning treachery. Rumours had spread throughout the army that the Byzantines were going to claim every place that they rescued from the infidels.

The sun was just beginning to warm the land where the Crusaders had camped for the night. The sky was a burnt orange as if it knew what was going to happen. A few men were up, stretching after a night in cramp shelters, their bodies silhouetted against the sun. A few birds sang and an early buzzard called as it soared in the warming thermals. No sound apart from the occasional clink of metal against metal of the Saracens could be heard but not loud enough for the Christian camp to take note. David brought their small fire back to life against the morning chill. He stared momentarily as over a rise the Saracens appeared, pouring over, reflecting the sun's morning glare. Rapidly he staggered to his feet shouting an order at Owen, "Get

Pierre up and fast."

He grabbed his saddle and threw it on to his horse's back and then did the same for his brother. He swung himself on to it. There was no time for reins. He had to hope his horse would listen to his spurs. Owen threw up a shield as he hurried to fetch weapons for Pierre. The Saracens were approaching fast on their horses. Infantry were gathering themselves into poorly ordered groups as Bohemond of Tarentum shouted, "This day, if it pleases God, you will all be made rich. Go forth and destroy all the infidels!" Those who were up, of the knights, stood as a wall against the Saracens so everyone else could get ready. Servants and the washerwomen were ordered to fetch water from the river for the fighters. None of the knights could take their eyes off the Saracens but only because the Saracens had the advantage of a larger army. All the Crusaders could do was hope that God was on their side and prepared to assist them in the destruction of the enemy. Some of the people not fighting fell to singing, praying and confessing their sins. Constance was not one. She knew she had to keep a straight head on her body to survive and help all those who were fighting the best way she could, by fetching water.

David soon found Pierre at his side with all his armour on unlike himself who was minus his protective leggings. Pierre was armed with spears and threw one to David to catch. There was a continuous rain of arrows and though their chain mail could stop most it couldn't stand the bombardment forever. Cries and grunts began to be heard from around David and Pierre but both stared straight ahead gulping and wishing they weren't in Anatolia. They glanced at each other and Pierre with his conical helmet on said, "Remember what we promised."

David nodded and pressed his knees tighter to the horse's side.

"We'll get out alive Davy."

"Of course we will," David replied as he raised the spear ready to charge it into someone's chest. He held on to it tight while adjusting the hold of his shield on his other arm. He was afraid but also he was beginning to feel the desire to get stuck in and kill the Saracens who were delaying their journey by getting in the way. He ducked as an arrow flew by too close for comfort and caught in the mail of the knight behind him though the man was not injured. For a moment he wished he hadn't been persuaded to travel to the Holy Lands as he looked to the man behind him.

A horn was sounded and some of the horses became more wide-eyed. At the back one reared up throwing its rider to the ground. The stallions snorted and quivered from the sense of Arab mares on heat. Spurs were dug into horses' sides and then all seemed to jump forward. Under the cover of longbow shots the cavalry of the Crusaders galloped towards the line of Saracen arrow wielding horsemen with lances and spears held horizontal so their sharp tips would bury themselves in the enemy's armour and body. David and Pierre instinctively threw their spears at the same time.

David's buried itself into the hard ground whilst Pierre's hit a Saracen who fell backwards off his horse with a scream of pain. David rapidly pulled out his sword to begin fighting the hoards off him as not all the Saracens were on horseback and already the footmen were around slicing at horses and men alike in the hope of some falling to the ground where they could destroy the Christians.

As the Christians approached the Muslims the mounted Saracens drew out their sabres for hand-to-hand combat. Crusaders fell from Saracen arrows but only because they were now at such close quarters. Meeting there were some discoveries for both sides on that both were wearing chain mail though not all of them were. Many were wearing padded leather coats, which was more flexible for firing arrows with. The Muslims wore boots and leather protection over their legs whereas the Christians had more chain mail. Helmets were not the same as the Saracens had turbans on their helmets over their coifs. Their shields were round but only because they used their bows more than the sword. Swords crashed together as well as on chain mail. Cloth and leather was torn as swords and sabres ripped through it. The brothers' hearts were beating the hardest they had ever done so from adrenalin and they gasped for breath as much as their horses. Time didn't seem to exist as they fought with the infantry finally getting involved. Through it all Pierre muttered, "I'll get through this; I will live for God is on our side."

David's mind was all on staying alive as much as his brother but he also appeared to be in the thick of it. With a booted foot he kicked out at one enemy as he fought another off with his sword before spinning round to swipe at the infantry man trying to drag him off his horse. The horse reared causing the Saracen to fall backwards and get trampled on by a mounted soldier from his own side. David was surrounded but he wasn't going to let that terrify him. He fought harder than he had ever done in his life and with more confidence than he had ever mustered before. He was surprising himself with the skills that had never been used apart from practicing with his brother and father.

They found themselves being pushed backwards into the river shallows where everyone was hiding if they weren't fighting. Though water was still reaching the knights and infantry in dribs and drabs the knights were sweating heavily under their mail and leather padding. Some were becoming disheartened and a few looked like they were about to surrender or faint away from dehydration.

The relief came at just the right moment, surprising the Saracens who had surrounded the Crusaders. With the arrival of the relief everyone who had been fighting for the last seven hours seemed to become rejuvenated especially as the Saracens began to gain heavy losses.

Seeing the new men Pierre charged forward again amidst the arrivals eager for more infidel blood to be spilt. His sword swung to the left and right almost hitting his horse's head a few times. His shield bashed into Saracen infantry breaking noses and ruining faces as he went. It was Bishop Adhemar who gave the last crushing blow to the Saracens. With his attack the Saracens turned and fled, leaving their camp completely and creating the prefect opportunity for looting on the Christian side.

There was noise all around them but only with the end did either really realise just how much there had been. There had been the cries from the Saracens as well as whistling as they attempted to terrify the Crusaders. In turn the Crusaders had been crying out their own threats. The air had been completely filled with the cries from both sides and within the battle there had been the swearing of the men as they fought hard with aching muscles, and hunger and thirst.

Bodies scattered the battleground and the injured were being brought off the parched rocky hillsides. David couldn't believe that they had won since there had been so many more Saracens. Silence seemed to fall with the night as the survivors sat round fires. For the younger knights such as David and Pierre they sat wide-eyed as all they had done sank in. Pierre rubbed at an arrow wound on his calf. The arrow had only got through since some links in the chain mail leggings had broken. David, it appeared, had come out unscathed whether to luck or God neither knew. David put his head in his hands making Pierre ask with concern, "Davy?"

"It was Hell, a living Hell Long-shanks. I can't go on, I've killed other men."

"You can go on; you know and I know you can. I didn't like it either but this is part of it. We are going to go to Heaven, don't forget that." Pierre got up and put a hand on his brother's shoulder, "We can do this and get through it together. Together we will be stronger because we are blood brothers and because we are close." David gave him a tight smile, "Thanks. I feel slightly reassured."

"Don't let anyone know your fear or we'll be the laughing stock." Pierre said fiercely and sat back down and rubbed at his wound with a scowl on his face.

"I can't believe we won Long-shanks."

"God was on our side once we had confessed our sins. From now on we will always have God on our side. We have had a victory today Davy and we had the first of our rewards."
"We are not close to Jerusalem though. We haven't rescued the city yet." David pointed out.

"We'll get there don't you fear, now shut up." Pierre said with slight annoyance.

David slept through the night but waking up in the morning and leaving the tent he stopped in his tracks. There were still bodies scattered across the ground especially the horses. Scavengers were already picking out eyes and at bellies. He squeezed his eyes shut to try and get rid of the sight of the bodies but he couldn't. He stepped out to the battleground and walked between the corpses while trying to keep the bile down in his stomach. He found a few non-fighters scavenging through the Saracen camp in search of anything that had been missed by others.

The washerwomen scampered at the sight of David but once he was far enough away returned to wherever they were.

He returned to find Constance with hands on hips and demanding, "What were you doing out there?"

"Taking control of myself. I will now be a hard man who does not let his emotions get in the way of his fighting."

"Don't change completely otherwise you wouldn't be you." She said with slight fear.

He eyed her suspiciously, "What made you say that?"

"I… You are my sweet friend and you wouldn't be the same if you went all the way.

Long-shanks is the hard one as you put it and you are the sensible caring one." "Maybe that is where I was going wrong then." He suggested.

"I like you as you are Davy and I'm sure there is a woman out there who would feel the same if she was allowed to marry you." "You." He teased with a smile.

She gave him a tight smile, "Not me."

"Anyone you plan to marry then?"

"No one I know of."

"What about me or Long-shanks?"

"Neither of you because you are like brothers to me even if we aren't blood related."

"But if you had to." He persisted.

"I couldn't choose now Davy. If I picked Pierre you would be jealous and if I picked you, you would be embarrassed and

Pierre would be jealous. This is silly, lets change the subject."
"If you want. What's for breakfast?"

"Whatever we have." She said and headed to the tent to see what there was otherwise there would be three grumpy men. All they had was stale bread and she knew that Owen would soon find his way over to the women to finish their scraps. For such a skinny man he never seemed to stop eating.

Chapter 6

Coming to the third village in two days after they had got back on the road Pierre moaned at the sight of the blocked up well and burnt crops, "I'm hungry and thirsty and all because of the stupid infidels. Look, go away!" He kicked out at a villager who was pleading for help with open hands, palm up.

"They can't help it as they are suffering as well; more so since we will just move on with the morrow leaving them with this mess."

"They are our allies so of course they will suffer. Go away!"

"I have no money." David tried to calmly explain at a woman tugging at his leg,

"We don't have enough food and water ourselves."

"There must be a stream around here." Pierre remarked as he stood up in his stirrups.

He couldn't see far so dropped back into his saddle with a grunt.

"They wouldn't be begging from us if there was Longshanks." David pointed out.

"We need water for the horses if we are to get to the Holy Lands." Pierre reminded his brother. Down at a villager he asked, "Water, where can we find it?"

The villager continued to talk in his own language babbling his pleads, set on his own agenda making Pierre kick out at him. The man neatly side-stepped and moved on to the next Crusader.

"I want to get to Jerusalem now so at least then there will be no more travelling." Pierre moaned as he spurred his horse forward, "I'm sick of this heat and the lack of water and food."

"And I was the one who didn't want to come to begin with." David commented with a smile as he caught up with his brother.

"Yes, well, I didn't realise it was going to be like this."

"Not enjoying yourself then?" David teased

Pierre shrugged his shoulders, "To be honest I thought the journey would be a lot easier then this and I didn't expect to be helping the emperor regain whatever land they lost to the infidels. Why should we be helping him anyway? It was his bloody fault if he lost land and cities to them. If we hadn't helped him we would be able to travel peacefully through this land instead of getting ambushed and almost routed by them."

"Everyone else is on our side."

"That's all fine and dandy but they don't have any food or water."

"Pray for some cooling rain then."

"Have you got nothing to say on the matter?"

"I feel you have said everything that I would say."

"That's the problem with being brothers." Pierre said in annoyance.

"My apologises for being from the same blood then." David replied with a slight bow of the head to hide the smile of merriment.

To see his brother reacting like so was quite amusing though it was only him grumbling away. It was true, however, that Pierre had voiced everything that he was feeling at that moment in time. It had always been that way; one of them was often to be found voicing the other's opinion without really realising they were doing it. Even he was becoming a little sick of all the travelling on horse back and though he was use to riding he was becoming saddle sore and he wanted to sit at least on a stool or bench instead of on the ground. He also wanted to sleep in a proper bed again even if the one at home had been a straw mattress. He closed his eyes and thought of that bed for a while until he was jogged back to the present as his horse stumbled on a rock. He sighed heavily, "Home, that seems like a distant dream somehow now."

Looking around the arid countryside of Anatolia it was completely different to what he knew from home. They marched and rode through the middle of the country in an area that didn't see a huge amount of rain as it was in the shadow of mountains to the east and north. The pale yellow parched ground was spread with rock and the dry withered bushes that was called food to the splattering of goatherds watched over by shepherds and their sons. There was green around springs or natural water gathering points from when rain did come.

It was a great contrast to their homeland of England, which had always been green, and in the autumn a warm red, gold and brown as the trees died down for the winter. There was also the rain and though there had always been a moan about it at home, here, in the middle of Anatolia there was a desire for it. They wanted to feel the wet cool drops on their brown or burnt dusty skin and for it to be felt trickling down their necks, washing away the sweat of several hundred men walking and riding as well as making the equine beasts shine again.

He wanted to see all the bright colours of home again as well as his parents. He wanted to stop squinting into the bright sunlight that was reflecting off the ground and to be able to stop quietly weeping from dust in his tired eyes and not be able to taste dust in his mouth. His mouth salivated at the thought of the meads, crude wine and small beer that was in the barrels back home. He wanted to be able to sleep properly through a night instead of suffering the muggy evenings and then the cold temperatures of the night.

"I suppose so." Pierre answered glumly, "We've been travelling for a year now and there is a chance we may not see home again."

"Wasn't it you who suggested the pact?" David pointed out.

"It was you who set us out on this morbid tone." Pierre answered sharply, "We are going to stop it right here."
"Fine."

"We will ride on in silence unless you can come up with a better topic of conversation." Pierre ordered with the authority of the older brother.

David decided that there was nothing to be said on that and remained silent. His brother was generally the one to have the last say. It had become a habit a long while back, one, which was unlikely to be broken like Pierre's seemingly constant need for making pacts. It was as if he wasn't always the confident one and actually needed David there to make him look like the older, braver confident son and to make him feel complete inside. As men they could work apart but as brothers they were close and worked together a lot better. If one was wanted then the other generally came as well. As they had been equal as sons and were close in age with no other siblings to play with they could share things they had including worries and secrets.

Whatever Pierre had said he ignored himself as he remarked, "By the time we get to Jerusalem there's going to be no one left if we have to carry on fighting these devil men."

"I thought we were changing the subject?" David enquired as he glanced at his brother.

"You were making the air around us down heartening, I was not." Pierre answered with a sniff and a raise of his chin. "What if I say I'm sick of your moaning?"

"I'm not moaning. I'm being observant."

"Can't you do it quietly then?" David was beginning to get irritated by his brother.

"You are becoming ratty." Pierre observed since David rarely got angry.

"Blame this heat and you then." David snapped before urging his horse forward to get away from his brother.

It was a gradual change but it was only when they came over a hill that they all realised what had been occurring. They had all become accustomed to the arid background of their travels that most had turned a blind eye on it. Coming over the hill they found themselves looking on to fertile farming land, which was obviously well irrigated.

Ahead of them was the walled city of Iconium. The Crusaders ignored the city to begin with since all they wanted was a drink. Reaching a well the people at the front of the column crowded round it and began drawing up water some for themselves while others thought first of their horses. Further back everyone else had to wait to satisfy their thirsts as well as the motley crew of mules, goats, horses and dogs that had become the Crusaders' pack animals as dead ones were replaced while travelling through Antaloia. For the last month of travelling they had all been attempting to survive on water from the sparse streams but with a large group of horses and people they quickly became dusty and stirred up so only the horses drank.

While waiting their turn Constance looked to the city with its few minarets standing tall above the other buildings and higher then the city's walls. From David she asked,

"What is this place?"

"Don't know." He looked to it as well.

"Iconium, that's what it is called." Pierre answered for them as he appeared leading his horse. He held out a waterproofed skin of water, "Take this and drink your full."

"Thanks." David smiled and took it from his brother. He gulped the cool water down like he had never drunk anything so sweet in his life. He didn't care that some ran down from the corners of his mouth and down his neck in his hurry to refresh himself. Finally he passed it to Constance as what water he hadn't drunk evaporated leaving muddy smudges on his skin. He brushed his cracked lips dry with the back of his hand and sighed, "I needed that. How did you get it so quickly?"

"Pushed my way through. That is what makes us different Davy. You are willing to be nice and wait but I like to make my presence known." Pierre commented proudly.

"Do you know what's going to happen with the city then?"

"I hope we are to plunder it. These Saracens deserve to lose it all since they are stopping us Christians from getting to our Holy City."

"I have heard that they consider it holy themselves." Constance put in cautiously as she stopped drinking just to see how Pierre would react. She didn't believe it to be true either but was in a contentious mood.

"Who said you could speak out?" Pierre demanded of her. She bit her bottom lip and bowed her head before replying, "Sorry sir."

"Don't do that again. Jerusalem a Holy City for them, now that's a load of codswallop. They are heathens and don't know a thing about religion, why would they have anywhere sacred but perhaps a pile of rocks?" Pierre voiced his opinion loudly and forcefully in the hope of passing it on to another person like Constance,

"Jerusalem is our Holy City and no one else's understand Constant."

"Yes sir."

"Good."

David looked on in silence knowing that it was likely he would get her moaning when alone. Whenever she was told off she always moaned to him about it and he always had to point out to her that she was the one who had wanted to become disguised as a servant and didn't want Pierre to be told. He was still waiting for the time his older brother would find out the truth.

After everyone had finally had their fill the army of Crusaders and their followers continued on to Iconium. The city residents weren't exactly the most welcoming of people nor did they show any signs of complete hatred. It was as if it was a common occurrence to see an army pass through the city's walls. No orders had been sent by Kilji Arslan and they were poorly garrisoned so the city easily fell under the control of the Crusaders. Since there was no reason to remain in the city of now friendly Armenians the Crusaders moved on towards Heraclea.

Just before reaching Heraclea they came up against the Saracens again. They could be seen from a short distance away and the Saracens this time round were in the minority. Both sides looked a little shocked to see the other but quickly recovered and dispersed into wings to battle it out. Some of the Crusader knights and infantry were sent to the back to watch over the non-combatants. The Saracens planned to have no similar failure and thrashing as outside Dorylaeum and the Crusaders were eager to prove themselves the better fighting force all over again.

At an order from both sides arrows began to fly through the air from the European longbows and the shorter curved bows of the mounted Islamic archers. A horn was sounded from the back and the knights charged forward with David and Pierre amongst them ready to prove their prowess to Robert Curthose, the man who was their leader. Nothing was going to stop them in once again defeating their enemy. Pierre vanished into the midst of the fighting with yells of, "for Jesus Christ!" and a sword held high until he thrust it down on the head of a Saracen with his hilt causing the Saracen's ears to start ringing under his helmet and slip sideways off his horse with his shield hand to his head. David found himself on the fringes fighting those who were cowardly or were attempting to escape. Many dodged his blows but others did not. He barely noticed when an arrow flew close to this arm, grazing it.

Thankfully this time round less men were lost and the fighting didn't last all day. Though they were weary from travelling that seemed to get forgotten as the adrenalin appeared in their racing bloodstreams.

Before long Saracens appeared to be quietly creeping away leaving the last gallant few to fall under the arrows and swords of the Europeans. There was relief for the end of the fighting, for now, but also a fear that the Saracens could return with reinforcements and begin the skirmish all over again.

Finding each other the brothers leant across while on their horses and gave the other a hug and Pierre with relief said, "I'm glad to see you alive."

"No more injuries I hope." David said with a smile.

"I haven't but by the looks of it you have." Pierre pointed to his brother's arm. David looked to his right arm and saw the wound he already knew about. Some of the rings on his mail had stretched apart under the strain of daily wearing and riding leaving his forearm a target for enemy weapons.

Across his arm was a large bleeding gash. To his brother David replied, "It's not too bad. It won't stop me from riding I don't think."

"You'd best get it seen to."

"A bit of bandage is all I need. Come on, lets find out where Constant and Owen have set up our tent. I don't know about you but I feel like some of my limbs are about to drop off from exhaustion. It's been a long day and all I want to do is eat if we have anything and sleep ready for another day of riding tomorrow." David turned his horse around and headed up to the camp that was being set up before his brother could say anything in reply to his comments.

Slipping off his horse David dropped to the ground and leant forward enough for his hauberk to slip off as Constance pulled it off him. He sighed with relief as the weight was dragged off him and he removed the undershirt. As he took a better look at his arm wound Pierre finally appeared and said, "They are putting several sheep together and making a feast of them. Are you going to come?"

"I'm not that stupid that I would say no to such an offer. I'm amazed they could find sheep fat enough for cooking." David answered as he let Constance wrap up his wound. While he was being tended to Pierre slipped off his horse and had Owen help him out of his mail. David added as an afterthought, "I'm starving, I'm glad they decided to do it. Who ordered it anyway?"

"Don't know." Pierre shrugged his shoulders, "Come on, the first one must nearly be done and I'm as hungry as you so much so I would eat my horse if there was nothing else."

"And that would be clever wouldn't it?" David remarked with a smile and shake of his head in amusement, "You would never get anywhere then would you? I wouldn't let you ride mine either."

"Brotherly love doesn't go that far then?" Pierre answered good-humouredly. He held out a hand and pulled David up on to stiff legs. With an arm round his brother's shoulders he led the way to the jointed sheep turning over the camp's central fire.

Pierre returned to their tent earlier then David who had fallen into conversation with a fellow knight and his arrival at the tent surprised Constance. Seeing Pierre enter she tried to cover up her breasts with fear. He stared at her, shocked, before saying, "I knew you were familiar all along. How could you Constance? All this time. You shouldn't be here at all and you know it."

She pulled on her shirt before retorting, "You never noticed."

"If a Priest realised they would put you down as a witch you realise. How did you do it?"

"On my own."

"No you couldn't. I may not have realised but Davy would have with his sharper eyes. Come on, out with it."

"You can't send me home now, we are too far for that." She pointed out.

"I'm going to speak with Davy on this." Pierre turned and left the tent leaving Constance feeling afraid. Making a decision she hurried after him so she could find out what David would say and to hope it didn't explode out of all proportions.

Reaching the fire Pierre took a tight hold of David's arm and said, "A word with you."

David looked up, "What's wrong?"

"A private word David and now." His eyes sidled to where Constance was standing nervously and David's eyes

followed. His eyes widened and he hurriedly stood up and allowed Pierre to drag him away. Back at their tent Pierre demanded, "How could you?"
"She twisted my arm."

"Not that, but not telling me. How come you didn't trust me?"

"She didn't want me to tell you; ask her." He gestured to Constance.

"You are so weak."

"Am not." David protested, "She told me not to tell so don't blame me."

"You could have just ignored that; we share everything remember."

"Not this though and I promised and you can't break a promise and you know that." David pointed out fiercely, "This is now between you and Connie so leave me out of it." He began to leave but Pierre grabbed hold of him and snapped, "You aren't going anywhere; you are staying put." "Careful, that's my injury Long-shanks. I'll stay but leave me out of this."

"Whatever." Pierre said distractedly as he turned to Constance and demanded, "Why Constance, why?"

"Because you would stop me from coming."

"That is true and it would have been the right thing."

"It's too late now." She pointed out stiffly again.

Pierre turned to his brother, "This is a mess, what should we do?"

"Everything would have been fine if you hadn't come in." Constance stated.

"Shut up Connie, its because of you that we are in a mess. You shouldn't have come.

A woman shouldn't be here, involved." Pierre snapped as he turned back to her. "What about those others then?" She asked, pointing out to him the fact that there were women who were along for the ride thinking it would be entertaining as well as for the washing and cooking, "There are children as well."

"Some, like Baldwin's, were foolish to have come. Look at her, she's ill half the time."

"I'm stronger then her." Constance said in defence.

"You still should have been sensible and stayed at home with mother."

"And get bored silly and die of worry for you two, no thanks." She retorted stubbornly, "I'm happier here, watching over you two."

"We don't need watching over; we aren't children Constance."

"What about Davy's wound then?"

"Leave me out of this." David put in from where he sat on the ground watching brother and cousin arguing. He had suddenly become immensely interested in his wound and was busy prodding it out of a childlike fascination of blood and holes in his body.

"You aren't getting out of this." Pierre warned as he turned to look at his younger brother.

"Why don't we just pretend nothing has happened, make no big thing about it and send her to be with the other women where she will be safe." David suggested calmly having dragged himself away from his scabbing wound. He wasn't going to let Pierre's anger get to him.

"How can you remain so calm?" Pierre demanded in annoyance.

"Because you are being so angry." David answered, remaining calm still but producing a smile from amusement, "Someone's got to keep a clear head over this and you certainly aren't."

"It's not a smiling matter David."

"I apologise then." David bowed his head to hide the smile that remained on his face.

"Hmpfh."

"There's nothing you can do Pierre." Constance put in causing Pierre to turn and the confrontation began to happen all over again as he replied, "There will be something so you just get ready for that moment."
David sighed, "Can we deal with this tomorrow? She isn't going anywhere and she may as well stay with us. I wouldn't trust her anywhere else in this camp especially with all these men."

"I've handled myself well so far since you were the one who told me to stay with the women." She retorted and turned to glare at David.

"You what?!" Pierre couldn't believe what he had just heard, "if they knew there was an unmarried young woman here she would be jumped upon from all sides and that would be the end of her modesty and marrying prospects. Did you go insane?" "She was meant to be hiding from you. There are plenty of women around and she can look after herself." David declared.

"From now on she is to stay with us." Pierre announced decisively.

"I'm safer helping you then being a sitting duck at the back." Constantine added as an extra reason to stay.

"No more needs to be said." Pierre said with warning.

She looked sullen from being told off by Pierre though she had been helping him convince David to let her stay with them rather than with the other women.

"Sound more grateful will you." David remarked with a frown, "He didn't have to be nice."

"Thank you then." She gave David a sickly sweet smile grudgingly.

"That's better." David answered, ignoring the sarcasm that had been evident in her actions.

Stopping for another night on the trail David found himself unable to sleep especially as he had been dozing on his horse from the heat and drudgery of long days in the saddle. There was also the ache of his healing wound that was making itself impossible to ignore at the moment. He wandered through the camp, passing the dying fires and the sentries who were staring out into the surroundings with boredom.

He and them seemed to be the only humans alive under the clear starry night sky. There were movements of others turning in their sleep and horses shuffling their positions as well as faint sounds of fires falling into themselves. Never, on his wander, did he expect to hear loud voices of an argument. He was surprised that the whole camp hadn't been disturbed by it but there again most had been tired enough to be oblivious to anything happening around them.

David stopped where he was as he felt it was supposed to be a private conversation though it didn't sound like one. He should have turned and returned to their tent but he was intrigued by what was being said. It seemed all the leaders were together arguing out some issue that appeared to concern all the Crusaders, the Byzantine guides. They were split down the middle with some wanting to get rid of the guides and others having no wish to. Tancred was all for losing each and everyone of the guides, "All they've been is trouble. They are working with the infidels, against us and have always done so."

"Where's your proof of that? You have caused trouble for them as well, hitting out at the Emperor's son." Bohemond remarked.

"If it wasn't for you we would have lost at Dorylaeum." Tancred returned fiercely. "I'm with him and you have been suspicious of them as much as your nephew here." Baldwin of Boulougne put in.

"Calm down, there is no real need for all of this." Adhemar, Bishop of Le Puy, an equal with all the others in every sense though he was a religious man.

"Come on, they can not be trusted. They routed half of my men." Raymond of Toulouse, the eldest of the Crusaders there, exclaimed, "And you, Adhemar, should know that since you were with me."

"It can't be all their fault. I know Nicaea was something we weren't planning but after that the Saracens would obviously want revenge." Robert Curthose commented. "You didn't like that bloody emperor after they took Nicaea and wouldn't let us plunder it." Tancred retorted.

"That was then and this is now." Robert returned.

"We can't get rid of them because they know this place better then us." Adhemar remarked calmly, the calmest of all the leaders, "We shouldn't be letting this tear us apart. We are all here for one thing, to return Jerusalem to a safe city for pilgrims and to make it Holy once again as the death place of our Lord Jesus Christ." There were grumbles at that short speech and silence as they tried to think of something to follow Adhemar. What he had said had reminded them why they had joined the Crusade. Tancred was the first to finally speak again, "If they are staying then I'm going. You take heed, you'll all end up dead." He got to his feet.

"Go then and good riddens." Robert said fiercely.

"I'm going with you." Baldwin announced and stood as well, "I can't trust those guides and they don't deserve our trust. You are falling straight into their trap. Ask Curthose here, he's in league with them." He pointed an accusing finger at the Duke of Normandy. Everyone turned to see how he would defence himself over such an accusation. Robert glared at Baldwin, "That is a lie, take that back." He got to his feet with clenched fists, "Are you willing to fight to protect such a lie."
One corner of Baldwin's top lip curled upwards in a sneer, "I am because I know that what I say is true. I know you made an oath to that Emperor so you will always be safe."
"Liar!" Robert hissed.

"Am I? My, my, what a temper." Baldwin teased, wanting to wind the Norman Duke up.

"I'll get you." Robert leapt forward to attack the Frank. Before he could even hit the other he was dragged away making him snarl in annoyance. He was held down while Raymond said sternly to the two traitors of the cause that they were already beginning to be seen as, "Leave this circle now, both of you. You are no longer welcome. I don't want to see you again. Leave quickly tomorrow and don't you dare try to persuade others to go with you. Take your people only. Both of you are traitors to the cause, traitors." Raymond ended with a hiss, "I hope you both end up rotting in Hell." "Come on Tancred." Baldwin took Tancred's arm and drew him from the circle of leaders. They passed by David who shrank into the shadows so he wasn't caught listening in on the conversation.

Realising that he had heard all there was to hear David turned and returned to his and Pierre's tent. All the

excitement seemed to have made him tired. He pulled off
excess clothes and then sat down and slipped in beside Pierre
who demanded,
'Where've you been?"

David was about to answer but he heard Pierre go on,
"Doesn't matter, bet you were with the dogs. We should take
them out hunting tomorrow."
David smiled; Pierre was talking in his sleep. He turned on to
his side and closed his eyes as he pulled some of the blanket
over to his side.

Pierre was the first up with the morning. He saw
Tancred and Baldwin leaving with their men and thought they
were leaving early to get some piece of glory first. He rushed
back to the tent and shook David hard, "Come see this. There
are bastards out there after all the glory for themselves."
Groggily David sat up, "What are you talking about? What's
going on? Are we packing up?"
    "Not yet but there are men on the move already. Come and
see it."
    "They are supposed to be leaving."
Pierre dropped to the ground, "What do you mean?"

    "Last night I was wandering; I couldn't sleep. I heard all our
leaders having an argument; by the way don't breath a word
of this to anyone and me telling you otherwise I could be in
serious trouble."
    "I won't." Pierre answered as he leant in closer to hear what
David had heard in the night just past.
    "Check that no one is outside." David instructed as he
looked round the tent fearfully.
Reluctantly Pierre did as he was told and got to his feet. He
walked right round the tent before returning, "No one there."
"Good, come here then."

The elder brother crouched down, "Come on then, do tell."

David glanced round again before saying, "Two of them left, Tancred and Baldwin, because they don't trust the guides we have. They've been labelled as traitors to the cause by the others so from now on you should keep your mouth shut on your opinions of the guides." He said it all seriously in a hushed voice. Pierre's eyes widened but nodded his head. "Not a word remember." David hissed and then got up.

Neither of them said anything when others observed that their numbers had shrunk. Their leaders were none the wiser about someone having listened and said nothing to their men about absent friends and comrades who had been with Tancred and Baldwin. Curiosity over those that had left didn't last more than a couple of hours since other topics of conversation came up or men decided to preserve their energy for another day of walking or riding.

Chapter 7

More ships loaded with men arrived, catching up with the Anglo-Normans who had arrived eight days earlier. From their own ship Pascal and Gallien looked across at them with father muttering, "Took their time."

"Bad winds." Gallien suggested brightly and only because the ships weren't sailing anymore and his stomach was feeling better with having the ships anchored close to the shoreline.

"We shouldn't be here, we should be going to the Holy Lands."

Gallien frowned as he looked at his father. Pascal's hands clutched tight to the side of the boat as if he was feeling frustrated. In fact Pascal was desperate. He wanted urgently to get to Jerusalem to find out if he had an uncle there or not and then be able to get rid of the burden of the sealed letter. Over on the shore sat the large city of Lisbon surrounded by high defensive walls with a walled citadel atop the hill. The Tagus River ran pass on one side. Steeples as well as a minaret or two stood tall above the hidden crowded buildings of the city.

The ships had previously pulled into Porto, driven in by a storm where Afonso Herinques had come to speak to their leaders seeking help to take Lisbon back from the Moors in exchange for anything they could take. He had shown himself worthy of help having previously taken other Moor held cities on the Iberian Peninsula. This was why they were anchored offshore from the city.

With the others arrived it was decided that after the midday meal everyone would land. The ships were run up on to the beach once dinner had been eaten. All the soldiers were armed with swords and axes in hand and dressed in their chain mail. Above them on the sandy hills the Moors were waiting for them, black Muslim Africans dressed in armour similar to that of the Normans and holding sabres and curved bows.

The Normans charged up the beach to the enemy with heads down and shields held half over their faces in the hope of escaping the flying arrows. For a brief while the two sides fought with swords clashing together and glinting in the bright summer sunlight. Under their armour and leather padding the Normans sweated away and it dripped down from under their helmets and down their foreheads. As Pascal and Gallien ran up the beach both brushed the sweat from their foreheads automatically though their helmets were in their way.

Pascal swung his sword up and attacked the first Moor he came to. He shouted at the black man, "Die infidel!" Their swords clashed against each other's shields before being thrown back from each other a step or two from the vibrations running up their arms. Each steadied and leapt forward again. This time the swords screeched together, edge running against edge. As the moor lifted his arm to strike again Pascal pushed home his small advantage. He smashed his shield boss into the moor's chest causing the black man to fall down. It was then that Pascal's sword thrust itself deep into the enemy's neck. The moor scrabbled at the hole in his neck where blood was burbling out. He was going to drown in his own blood but already Pascal had moved on, stepping over the withering body.

Gallien took a step backwards as he came before the enemy, a tall black man who was sneering, revealing white teeth in his mouth. Gallien found himself freezing and his arms becoming so feeble that he had to use both hands to hold his sword but even that wasn't enough. His father was close by, thankfully, and saved him from being slaughtered. It brought him out of his trance and he caught sight of his father giving him a tight reassuring smile before returning his sights on the killing of Moors.

It was not long before the Moors turned in a trick move in the hope of luring the Crusders further away from the safety of their ships and their fellow soldiers so they would be individually picked off. Saher of Archelle saw what was occurring and ordered the Normans to come away from the gate leading to Lisbon's outskirts spoiling the fun of the Moors.

With them away orders were made to pitch the tents on the hills looking across to Lisbon. By the evening only the two main leaders had tents on the shore. Everyone else was off shore in the boats feeling safer there then on land where the Moors could ambush them. Pascal and Gallien were thankful to be on board instead of being on the watch of thirty-nine men back on shore.

Gallien was in shock from his first real experience of fighting. He sat against the mast actually shivering from the shock. Pascal looked down at his son with concern. Though he felt concerned he found himself snapping, "snap out of it. You are a grown man. Behave like a Renard. Remember you were trained to fight like this. Your grandfather fought the infidels bravely and your great grandfather came over with King William the Bastard. There are no cowards in this family and don't you dare change that tradition."

"I…" Gallien attempted to explain himself but then bowed his head as he said, "I will do better next time."

"Pray to God that you get a second breath of courage for this fight is not over yet. This is likely to last a few weeks at least. I want you able to use your sword again understand and without hesitation."

"Yes father." Gallien's head remained low from his shame of having frozen at the first sight of the enemy. He had imagined them to be ugly demon like things so had therefore been surprised to find them as human as himself and his father though with a different skin colour. In fact he had been slightly turned off at the thought of having to kill his fellow men whether he had been trained to or not. He had to force a reminder on himself that they believed differently to Christians and had no God. The only relief Pascal had for being stuck in a potential siege with Moors was that King Alfsonso of the Portuguese was promising them the chance to plunder Lisbon once it had been reclaimed. For a moment as he looked out to sea he wished he had a brother with him to confined in instead of his son. Over the years in fact he had prayed desperately to God for a brother or at a pinch a sister but neither had appeared. He wanted a brother who he felt equal to and who he could easily talk to. There had been no one he could argue with and only the village children to play with but his mother had disapproved of that. It had been a lonely childhood.

October 1097

From the hillside where they set up camp for the night the Crusaders could see the city of Antioch. It sat proudly on its hill surrounded by its high walls which ran along one ridge of Mount Silpius, around the foot of it and then parallel to the Orontes River. Already they had captured some forts further out from the city so that if a siege began the camp wouldn't be attacked from behind. From a distance it appeared impossible to attack with no way to even get close to or inside it. Some feared, including the Renard brothers, that they would end up in a siege again though this time there were no Byzantines of any high influence to stop them plundering once inside.

As people set up camp a horseman rode through two rows of tents straight to the centre and dropped down from the mare's back. Crusaders began to gather in the centre of the camp wanting to know why the rider was there. Whispers went round with men all having different theories on why the man had appeared. Their leaders all gathered in one tent and called the messenger in. Pierre pushed David forward, "You've got sharp hearing, go find out what is being said."

"Once was enough. If you really want to know then go listen yourself."

"You didn't get caught last time so you are unlikely to this time." Pierre hissed. "Go on Davy." Constance added, "Please." She looked pleadingly at him and with a sigh he went leaving her smiling triumphantly at his brother. Within the tent the messenger was standing before all the separate Crusader leaders, "... Through the prowess of our honourable leader Alexius Commodous the port of St Symeon has been secured."

"That's all very well and good but is he going to let us use it?" Raymond of Toulouse demanded, "Will we be able to use the port to get supplies to us? An army can't fight on empty stomachs; we need feeding you know."

The messenger stuttered an answer since he didn't really have one, "Yes... Yo...You will be able to get supplies."

"Good."

"The good Emperor believes a siege from a distant would be best."

"Advising us from afar now is he?" Bohemond sneered, "Has a crystal ball does he?"

"I think that is what should be done as well." Tatikios, the Byzantine representative and in charge of the Byzantine forces within the Crusader army, remarked with his nose in the air.

"I… I… Do… don't know sir."

"Of course you wouldn't." Bohemond returned, "And you Tatikios, we didn't ask for your advice."

"Bohemond don't terrify the poor man." Raymond said with warning, "All he can do is pass on whatever has been told to him. We don't need the Emperor's advice but only because he's not here. We are all sensible men and I'm sure we can make our own decisions." To the Messenger he said, "Go get something to eat and then you can head back on the morrow."

"Thank you sir."

At this point David slipped away to report back to brother and cousin who were impatiently waiting towards the back of the gathering. As he arrived back Pierre demanded, "Well?"

"Some port has been captured by Emperor Alexius Commodous."

"That it?"

"About it. Come on, I want something to eat if there is anything." David led the way from the centre of the camp with the other two following feeling disappointed that it was nothing else more exciting. Catching up with her cousin Constance asked, "What did they have to say about it?"
"Nothing really that interesting."

"Oh come on Davy, don't keep it all to yourself."

"There were comments made but they aren't really relevant to us."

"We don't care, tell us."

"No." David said sternly and sped up his walking.

He contemplated what had been said from a rock while looking at the city in the evening light. He felt that a siege from where they were wasn't very useful as they sat with only one view of the city and the city could get supplies through on the other sides unseen by Crusader eyes. It also wouldn't really worry the people of Antioch either while sitting on a hillside opposite as with the distance between them a proper battle could be created instead of the little outbreaks of fighting which would wear down the morale of the city. If the siege were from a distance it may allow the Byzantines, though highly unlikely, to make contact with Yaghi Siyan, ruler of Antioch, and come to a peaceful arrangement which would then create turmoil within the Crusader camp.

It appeared the leaders had spent most of the night debating the next stage in dealing with Antioch now they had reached the city. It had come out as a majority against one man, Tatikios. None of the Crusaders wanted to sit out the winter looking daft on the hillside with Yaghi Siyan jeering at them from the walls of Antioch. With the decision made and leaders told where they were to go the camp was taken down and moved to new positions closer to the city and its five gates.

The Norman Duke's men, including the Renard brothers and Constance, were set up alongside Bohemond in watching the Gate of St Paul. Raymond of Toulouse was outside the Dog Gate and Godfrey was to be found by the Gate of the Duke between the city wall and the river. Tatikios had his own men as far back as possible in the pretence of defending them from any attacks from the river valley. The Bridge Gate was unwatched by Crusaders since it had the Orontes River as protection.

Chapter 8

October 1147

Pascal winced as the jeering and catcalls from Lisbon's city walls started up for another day. Just the day before the crusaders had watched in horror as the Moors had desecrated the Holy Cross, pulled out of one of the churches. Feeling aggrieved by the action many wanted to attack there and then and end the siege. Thankfully they were calmed down before they got themselves killed..

Depending upon the mood of the camp anyone on a daily bases was left frustrated or hurt by the insults. Today was a day when Pascal was feeling like he was going to be easily wound up. He knew the insults being thrown down to him and the others watching the city were mainly lies, for himself anyway. He knew his wife would not sleep with anyone else and trusted her not to.

He rubbed a hand across his sunburnt tired face as a soldier sat down beside him. Admittedly the man was younger then the forty year old but not by much. The man, Turstan Clough, a man just shy of forty years, smiled, "They getting you down?"

"Yes. I'm trying to ignore them especially as I know Anne wouldn't do such a thing."

"I'm afraid to say that I worry. Isabella is a young woman and she has only given birth to one child. She is an obedient woman but I don't think I'll truly be able to trust her."

"I'm sure you can." Pascal looked to the man with his green eyes and dark brown hair. Sir Turstan was a short man compared to Pascal and was an Englishman married into Norman money and blood to save his small family manor from being taken. They wouldn't even still have it if his father hadn't supported the Norman invaders. Turstan smiled in amusement, "You don't know my Isabella. She lived in Normandy before she married me and some of their ways are different to the better behaved women of our beloved country."

"I suppose so. I don't think you were here to talk wives. What are you here for?" "Word is that the siege will end today." Turstan whispered after glancing round nervously. Pascal frowned, "Do our leaders support this?"

"Don't know but when everyone gets back we attack. People are getting sick of all this waiting."

"That includes me. I expected to be going to the Holy Lands and not getting stuck here even if they say we will still get to go to Heaven."

"We get to plunder the city as well though." Turstan remarked with eyes bright with the thought of the looting he could do, which he could then perhaps buy more land or use to make a worthwhile dowry for his daughter. "Whose idea is this then Turstan?"

"Will you join us?"

"I don't know." Pascal felt he should play safe since he wanted to get to the Holy Lands and Jerusalem. If he got himself killed he would never find out more on the uncle that may or may not be alive.

"Father!" Gallien ran up to them.

"What Gallien?"

"We are to attack tonight father and surprise them so we can take the city." "Where did you hear that?" Turstan asked with surprise.

"Everyone is talking about it." Gallien answered innocently, "Aren't you meant to be keeping watch?"

"We are." Pascal said with warning to his son who was over stepping the mark saying such a thing to his father.

"How about this though. The Flemish are unhappy with the King and his battle plans."

"The hostages?" Turstan asked.

"Them." Gallien eagerly replied with a smile. After his first meeting with the enemy he had recovered well especially when the Moors started attacking them almost daily once the camp had been firmly set up. He crouched down and whispered, "The

Flemish plan to kill the host…"

Pascal put his hand over his son's mouth and held it there firmly as he glanced round before hissing, "No more. If they think you are involved we will all be in trouble and I want to get to Jerusalem. Do you understand?"

Gallien drew his father's hand away with his two shaking ones, "I understand."

"Why do you so desperately want to get to Jerusalem?" Turstan asked, "You keep talking about getting there."

Pascal sighed and glanced at his son. Seeing his father's look Gallien got to his feet and left the two men though he would have liked to have remained and feel like one of the men instead of still feeling like a boy.

Turstan looked at his friend, patiently waiting for Pascal to speak. Pascal looked down at his feet for a moment before looking to his friend who had an expression of encouragement on his face. Turstan asked hopefully, "Well?" "My mother, before I left, gave me a letter telling me to give it to a David Renard if he lived." "If he lived?"

"Yes, he and my father were on the previous Crusade with my mother. They were separated in Jerusalem. She mentioned that he might be important to me." He frowned as he thought about it, "what do you think she meant by that Turstan?"

"Only God probably knows and this uncle if you ever get to meet him."

"How though? I have no idea what he looks like..." Before he could say anymore he looked up as he heard a noise. Turstan looked up and took hold of his sword as he stood. He remarked, "Trouble is brewing around here. It's been slowly building up and now it's finally revealed itself."

"It will be those Flemish. Can't they accept anything?" Pascal said as he stood as well. They saw the soldiers run from their camp across to King Alfsonso's camp where the hostages were. It was not long before the Flemish were clashing with the King's men in an attempt to get inside his camp. The two Normans looked down on the fighting and occasionally glanced to the city walls where the Moors were now shouting encouragement for the continuation of the fighting between allies. Turstan asked, "Should we try and stop this?"

"We are only two men and can't speak the language. They wouldn't listen to us anyway. We aren't important to them." Pascal remarked with a frown. The right thing to do would be to wade in but it would only get them killed. Sitting around being mocked by the enemy wasn't good for morale and even he was getting sick of all the sitting around for someone else's fight. Even he was starting to contemplate heading home after this rather than Jerusalem. Was a letter and a possible uncle enough to keep him pressing on?

"True."

"We should get back to watching the walls. The infidels may use this time of mayhem to attack us with all they've got."

"It would be better if they did rather then their sorties. We are weakening each other slowly; it's a waste of men doing it this way." Turstan said, expressing his opinion on the siege that to him had dragged on far too long.

"This is probably short compared to the ones my father experienced. He hated all the sitting and waiting especially when they ran out of food and water. My mother hated them as well."

"Your mother went?" Turstan was shocked as if he had forgotten Pascal had already told him that his mother had been on the first Crusade, "Married to your father I hope."
"Unmarried but she was with my father and I guess my uncle as well. She dressed as a man to go since she wasn't suppose to go."
He remembered her telling him about it when she was a child and as he grew older he hadn't believed her until his father reluctantly confirmed it. His parents had acted oddly with each other for a while after Pierre had confirmed the tales all to be true.

Both looked away from their conversation as orders were shouted below and order returned to the Crusaders as the Flemish leaders took control of their men. Sir Turstan remarked with relief, "I'm glad that's over. I wouldn't really want to have to go in and fight them and have my wife being told that I died not fighting the enemy but my allies."
"I don't think it would ever have come to that."

Word rapidly ran round that the siege was to end with the new day. Gallien was actually excited about it, hoping for some fighting, proper fighting and not just short skirmishes. As Turstan stirred up their small fire that evening he remarked to
Gallien, "I don't think there is going to be much fighting."

Gallien's face fell, "What do you mean? How do you know?"

"You obviously didn't hear." Turstan smiled, "It's to be peaceful. They've seen our tower and aren't going to be able to destroy that like they had with others. You'll have to wait until you reach the Holy Lands for some proper fighting I feel. Apparently the city is hungry and men can't live with an empty stomach."

The young man truly looked downcast then and to try and cheer him up the soldier added, "Don't worry, there's plenty of other things to do here, like plundering the city, we've been promised that much even if nothing else."

"That's not the same though." Gallien moaned and stared into the fire feeling down hearted.

"It's just bad luck that we can't fight them properly. It shows that they are cowards with no sense of endurance if they can't survive without food for less than six months. I heard that some of the sieges in the Holy Lands were a lot longer. It shows how much tougher we are than the Mohammeds. To be honest I'd prefer this ending peacefully without fighting as I'd like to live for most of the Crusade and we haven't even got to the Holy Lands yet."

"Are you going to carry on then?" Pascal asked.

Turstan looked at his friend and puffed up his chest, "of course. You?"

Pascal sighed, "I'm not sure at the moment."

January/February 1098

Winter was not going well. Death was stalking the camp as men died of starvation. The cold wet weather that had appeared and followed them down from Cilician Caesarea wasn't helping either. Desertions had begun and men of importance such as Peter the Hermit were dragged back by Tancred and put under watch. Foraging parties were often low on numbers since they no longer had the knights protecting them for they in turn had lost their rides from skirmishes and natural causes. David didn't actually know what others were doing but not wishing for him and his brother to lose their own horses to thieving horseless knights he decided that it would be best to guard them even when they were tied up close to their tent. He told no one of his plan until Constance came looking for him.

"Davy, I'm glad I've found you. Long-shanks…" She was smiling but that turned to a frown as she saw him sitting on a rock in front of their four horses with his sword resting on his lap. Like everyone else he was starting to look a little too lean. It was more noticeable in Pierre as he had always been thinner. Clothes hung off everyone now and David had had to cinch in his belt. The soldiers still had their muscle mass from training out of boredom more than necessity but the skin was taut over the muscles making them look sinewy. "David? What are you doing?"

"Guarding our horses."

"Why?"

"You know why unless you want to walk the rest of the way to Jerusalem. There are knights out there who have lost their own and may be tempted to take ours. Also everyone has empty bellies and might kill one for the sake of food whether it is someone else's or not."

"I suppose so. Should I tell Long-shanks?"

"Send him this way and I'll tell him."

Constance turned and headed off to find her elder cousin.

Pierre wasn't happy to be going to his brother and it sounded in his voice as he appeared, "Why couldn't you have come to me? What are you doing David?"   "Watching over our horses."

"Good, I'm not having someone take them from us. They may be getting money but that is nothing compared to a horse and I'm not having ours taken. We are knights and it isn't the same with no horse." Pierre replied as if he was standing at a pulpit giving a sermon to the sinners of the world.   David smiled, "Glad you agree."

"I'll do the evening and night if you want."

"That's all right then. I'm glad to see your spirits don't need rising since everyone else's do."

"I have heard news." Pierre smiled, "Something you have yet to hear first for once."

"Tell me then."

"Since people's spirits are low some events are going to occur."

"All we really need is food Long-shanks."

"God has left us, well that's what others think. What is to occur will let God know we still believe in Him so He will come back to us."

"I personally thought He was always with us."

"That is your opinion."

"What things are to happen then?"

"Sermons probably and pray."

"You weren't really listening were you?" David smiled in amusement. Pierre looked slightly annoyed that he had been found out and reluctantly admitted, "I wasn't really."
"Got you."

Pierre looked angrier and then headed away.

It seemed to lift some of the men's spirits having time to pray and being able to confess any long overdue sins. It wasn't, however, enough in Adhemar's view and he called for the removal of all women from the camp. He felt they were taking away the feel of the whole Crusade and were making it look more like a merry hunting party then an army with a very important mission. When hearing of the plan Constance was in a hurry to find her cousins. Finding them together, thankfully for her, she exclaimed, "You've got to help me."

Briefly she wondered why both were together in the tent but then remembered that Owen was watching over their horses.

"What have you done?" Pierre sighed.

"Nothing but be born a woman. The Bishop wants the women to leave and I'm not going. You've got to hide me."

"Remember they don't know that you are a woman."

"They are going to search the tents though."

"You aren't a woman to them." David said, repeated to get it into her panicking mind.

"They could find out and then... I'm dressed as a man, what would they think of me if they found out."   "They won't." David said fiercely.

"No one knows you as anything but a man so why would they suspect otherwise unless someone else has seen you getting dressed or...." Pierre didn't mention her messy time of the month since it wasn't really a man's place to talk about it and he was supposed to remain ignorant on it but that was hard since he now knew that

Constant was Constance, "Has anyone?"

"The women know." Constance looked at her feet as she spoke quietly in the hope that Pierre in his heightened state would not hear her and would carry on preaching.   "Hang on. When did they find out? Are any of them likely to tell?" Shaking suddenly at being caught out all over again she replied, "I don't know."   "Have you made enemies of any of them?" Pierre demanded, "Cause if they are forced to go then they will tell."

"Not that I know of."

"That's all right then." Pierre said with some relief though he didn't feel reassured by what Constance had said.

"I don't think the Bishop will get away with it anyway. There will be too many objections so you shouldn't worry so." David remarked to his cousin, "You are safe and the others probably also. There would be uproar from our leaders and well as the men, even you Pierre. I know where you go sometimes." There was a twinkle in David's eye as he finished his sentence.

"Hmpfh." Pierre glowered at his brother with arms crossed as he realised what he thought was secret appeared not to be so. He eyed his brother wondering whether he was better at hiding his own desires, if he had acted on them at all. "What if they find out who I really am though?" she asked desperately, turning the conversation back on her, "They could try me of... of..."

"There you go then. If you can't think of anything then they probably can't either." Pierre said confidently, "Just don't go and announce that you are a woman to any men and hope none of the women or children say anything and no one will notice.No one had so far. You've got away with it this long and I'm sure you'll get away with it all the way to Jerusalem. Take a deep breath, calm down and go and see if you can find some food."

Constance took a deep breath while looking to her two brothers.

"Calm?" Pierre enquired.

She nodded at him and he added, "Good, off you go then."
He gave her a smile and she scowled at him before leaving.

If that was not enough Pierre was fuming behind his beard a few days later. He dragged David out of the camp, away from their horses, and exclaimed, "Take a look at that, cowards."

Standing with other onlookers who were talking amongst themselves, David looked in the direction Pierre was gesturing in with a hand and saw Tatikios leaving with his men. Pierre went on, "They could never be trusted and look, leaving when it gets too tough for them. Weak, that is what each and every one of them are. They think we'll fail but I hope we can prove them all wrong."

"This won't help our fighting spirit. If they think its hopeless what will others be feeling?"

"They want us to lose don't they?" Pierre went on, ignoring David's comment. "Do you think they are in league with the enemy?"

"It could be said that they are wiser then us."

"Are you saying it was right for them to leave?" Pierre exclaimed in wide eyed horror.

"I'm not saying it was right." David answered defensively, "Am I ever going to be able to open my mouth without you objecting to what I say? I was just commenting. I wasn't saying I am on their side. I am here to rescue Jerusalem not to make myself look like a coward. Now, if you have finished accusing me of something I'm not I'm going back to guard our horses before someone takes them." He turned away and headed back through the camp. Pierre stood where he was for a moment and then hurried after David. He caught hold of the other's swinging arm but David threw it off. Pierre stopped where he was looking hurt as he called out, "I'm sorry." David didn't respond so the elder decided that he needed to let his younger brother calm down before trying to apologise again.

He had not planned to offend David but that was how it had come out meaning he was now annoyed with himself. He knew he had to stop trying to cause arguments between himself and David because each other was all they had apart from Constance. She didn't matter so much as she hadn't been part of their lives up until eight years ago when the brothers' bond was already firmly sealed and anyone new would find it hard to break in. He muttered to himself, "You are a fool, a stupid fool Pierre."

Bohemond called together all the knights that still had horses. Seeing the collection he couldn't believe that from such a large camp he had only seven hundred mounted knights. With such a small number he decided to bring them under his command. To them he addressed, "Gentleman a new force is heading our way in alliance with the enemy within the walls of Antioch. We must attack them; surprise them away from here to protect all the lives in our camp. If they reach us here we will not last. We will catch them before the Iron Bridge. With such a small force we must ambush them and because we have God on our side we will win." No one had any objections but David and Pierre glanced at each other. Pierre murmured, "Remember."

"I know. I think if we both live through all this mother and father will certainly be proud of us."

"Don't suggest we won't. We will." Pierre said fiercely.

"Of course. Come, we go tonight so we should get ready." David calmly replied in a soothing tone to placate his brother.

The seven hundred strong cavalry headed out as the night fell. In the place they chose the Saracens would become trapped between the Orontes River and Lake

Amik Gőlű and therefore would be an easy target and death would rapidly fall on the Crusaders' enemy. The Crusaders were split up into five squadrons to fight and a sixth to act as reserve. As they waited for the morning behind a low hill none could sleep, as they feared Ridwan of Aleppo's army would slip by. Pierre murmured a pray before he said to David, "Do your best and I'll do mine. Come out alive."

"Of course I will." David answered stiffly. "I know but…"

"But?" David tried his best to see what Pierre's face was telling him but he couldn't see it clearly from the shadows cast across his face.

"It wouldn't be the same without you." Pierre said carefully. He shifted uncomfortably, aware he was being foolishly sentimental, "we came together and it wouldn't be the same if you were to die."

"Hey. Even if we are to go to Heaven I'd prefer to either follow you or go with you."

David said with a tight smile into the darkness, "Has that made you feel better?"

"Thanks."

"You were the one who wanted to do this don't forget. I came with you because I had to. It's only because we are brothers and always end up doing everything together that I'm here. I would have been perfectly happy at home and finding an heiress and having my own little estate or maybe become a merchant." David couldn't help his frustrations to the siege, the crusade, even his brother from revealing themselves.

"Sssh." Someone hissed.

David added with a frown, "I'm going to try to sleep. Are you?"

"We are in the reserve aren't we?"

"I think so." David said as he lay down on his side and rested his head on his two hands, "You should try and get some sleep Longshanks. It could be a long day tomorrow."

As dawn arrived everyone got ready and held their horses' reins as still as possible while they sat astride them so the metal of the reins didn't jingle too much to warn the enemy. It was two hours after the sun had risen when Ridwan's army were heard to be approaching. The Crusaders waited patiently, a skill they had mastered a long while back; for the enemy to reach them before at Bohemond's word the five squadrons of knights descended on the vanguard of Ridwan's army.

The sound of clashing shields and swords began to ring out between the hills and echoed down the valley. From behind the hill the reserve watched as the Saracens panicked and dropped back to the main force entangling themselves up so much that they couldn't fight.

Through luck more than anything the army's leader shouted out orders and the troops turned and began to fight back. Though they were in the minority the Crusaders did not hesitant as their foe began to defend themselves and rapidly began to win. Before they were overcome by the enemy Bohemond and the reserve jumped into the disarray of fighting men and rearing horses. In the confined area the Saracens could not control their rearing animals and many turned their horses round. Herd mentality caused the riderless horses to follow suit. Ridwan followed his men's lead and returned to the safety of his city, Aleppo.

The crusaders didn't pause to catch their breaths as they pushed their horses after the riderless ones. With all the losses they needed to claim as many as possible and whatever supplies there were in the saddlebags. Others raided the bodies and another group went for the abandoned supply carts to get them moving towards their siege camp.

Chapter 9

English pride revealed itself in Gallien as he felt angry when he saw the Flemish entering Lisbon first. He turned to his father who was also one of the hundred and forty Anglo-Normans who were to enter the city and take the upper fortress peacefully. He demanded, "Aren't you going to go anything about this?"

"I maybe a soldier but I'm not one with any influence." His father pointed out calmly, "We must be patient." He looked up at Lisbon with its battered walls. Over the siege period the Normans had been trying to wear down the morale of the Moors with two trebuchets. All over the place there were holes in the tops of the walls and craters where the boulders had squarely hit the walls.

The Flemish allies entered boldly and with triumphant in their step but only because they had slipped in more men then their hundred and sixty. The Normans were led in by the Archbishop and his retinue of bishops and servants, holding a cross up for everyone to see. The men were quickly directed to positions, some to watch over the possessions being handed over by the Moors, some to the searching of homes and beheading those who had lied, and the rest to guard the city walls and the cross which had been put in the tower that stood highest above the city while the clergy prayed with others who were close by.

Pascal kept an eye on his son as they stood on duty by the church and its steeple. He could see he was itching to join the badly behaved Flemish and go looting. It hadn't been long until the testosterone had got the better of the allies and the

peaceful surrender had turned bloody with deaths everywhere. The moors were slaughtered as they left the city and few were lucky to escape the streets of hell with the jeering soldiers and their swords and maces. After so long with nothing to do Gallien had energy that needed to be expelled and Pascal knew that it would be best to keep him near so he didn't bloody his hands with sinful deaths. Pascal hissed, "Don't you dare. We are better than them and I'm not having you embarrassing our family. Think of God and Jesus. We will get our share for behaving and they are likely to lose theirs in the end. Think God and Jesus." He turned away from his son and looked to the cloudy sky. For a brief moment he closed his eyes but they sprang open as he heard heavy footsteps inside as if they were running. Both he and his son entered the large church where they knew the Lisbon Bishop was praying. They stared in shock. By the altar the elderly man lay on his back in his robes with blood pooling around him. Gallien looked to his father with wide frightened eyes, "What should we do?
Who would do such a thing?"

Pascal looked round and then ran to the Bishop with a hand on the hilt of his sword just in case the killers were still about. He heard a door swinging and ran to it. Looking out of it he saw a group of moors making a dash for it having taken their final revenge. Returning to the body he bent down over the body with its silt throat and stabs. Gallien hurried over to join his father. Pascal glanced up at his son, "He's dead. They all need to be told."

"We were meant to be watching him though."

"There's more than one entrance to this place." Pascal stood up.

"Who did it you think?"

"Men taking revenge for the slaughter outside." Pascal remarked dispiritedly and then stiffly added, "one of us needs to go and report this." He looked to his son. It was something his son needed to decide to get over his sudden fear, which he wanted gone as soon as possible. Gallien looked his father steadily in the eye but then they flickered to the corpse. He gulped, "You go for they won't listen to me."

"Are you sure?"

"I'll make sure none of them come back and do anymore harm." Gallien nodded, "go father, I'll stand right here." Pascal nodded in turn and after gesturing a cross over his body at the crucifix hanging above the altar ran out of the church to report the murder.

Before long the Flemish came to a halt in their pillaging and harassment. They asked their fellow allies to forgive them and help them look after the city while the loot was divided up and compensation dealt with. They were all feeling embarrassed for themselves since they had been shown up by their counterparts who had remained in control and had not allowed greed to get the better of them. There was disbelief in some that the Normans had been so restrained.

From above a gate the Renards watched with Turstan as the enemy filtered out. Gallien leant over and threw a piece of chipped wall down at them. Neither man stopped him from doing so since Turstan started up a conversation, "They've found food and the infidels claim it had gone sour and therefore had none."

"God had turned against them then." Pascal replied without looking at his friend.

"Their god you mean." Turstan corrected but then went on, "You know we will still get to Heaven for doing this. Once the winter ends I might just go home. Isabella can't be trusted. What are you going to do Pascal?"

"We go to Heaven?" Gallien looked at them, "Father, then there is no need to go on is there? Can we not go home?" "You are a Renard Gallien and we persevere. This is only the beginning of the
Crusade. We've begun and we must reach the end just as your grandfather did." Gallien looked annoyed at that, "I don't want to go on. We've done our bit, haven't we?" "Gallien!" Pascal warned.

"What?"

"There is the Holy Lands to rescue and we are going there after the winter has ended."

"What about our earnings?"

"That'll come with us."

"I like it here."

"You obey me as your father Gallien and you'll come with me. I don't want to hear anymore objections from you." Since he didn't want to find himself in the middle of a family argument Turstan attempted to change the conversation, "Dead and sick people were found in that temple of theirs." "Mmm." Pascal answered distractedly. Turstan fell silent with a sigh.

June 1098

Their allies, the Armenians, captured Harem allowing supplies to finally get through safely. With that as encouragement a tower was built to block the Bridge Gate so that supplies from St Symeon were also protected. Within Antioch Bohemond made contact. Word got round that the Saracen ruler of Mosul, Kerbogha, and his allies were approaching to aid his comrade Yaghi Siyan. A decision was made on whether to use the inside contact.

Constance was afraid that this time would be the end of it for everyone concerned and tried to persuade the brothers to leave. Just for once she was terrified. She tried to talk David round first with no luck, "Davy, I don't think we should stay.
We won't be able to fight them. I hear there is a lot more of them then there are us.

We can't face them in battle; there aren't enough riders. We will get slaughtered."

"Constance you came willingly though we told you it would be hard and dangerous. Neither of us are leaving and don't bother trying Pierre for you'll get an earful from him about honour and God being on our side."

"You've tried?" She looked hopefully at him.

"No and I won't. I'm not going to be named a coward for running when we were needed most. Anyway I have heard we are to attack the city with inside help. Once within those walls we will be safe and our patience rewarded."

"The infidels will still be here though, they'll besiege us." She wailed at him.

"Stop behaving like a woman. It's your fault you are here."

"You should have stopped me harder."

"Would that really have worked?" He asked with raised eyebrows.

She looked to her feet and sulkily answered, "No."

"There you go then. We are staying and that's final."

"Cowards!" Pierre shouted as he appeared in the tent.

"More deserters?" David enquired calmly and warned Constance not to try or say anything with a glare at her.

"A whole load of them. If this goes on there will be no one left and how then will we attack Antioch." He said so loudly that David and Constance felt the whole camp would have heard. Dropping to the ground he said more quietly, "I have heard rumours that we are to attack tonight."

"And where did you hear this?" Constance asked, eyeing him.

He shrugged his shoulders.

"Who's gone?" David asked.

"Stephen of Blois. He's going to miss out on all the fun."

"I wouldn't say killing men and horses was fun." Constance remarked with a frown.

"This is war Connie, remember that. It's meant to be brutal." Pierre reminded her.

"I don't know why you men like to fight; couldn't you have just talked about it." "That's something only a woman would say." Pierre commented and then with a smirk said, "Best not let the Bishop hear you say something like that." For a moment she looked like she would kill him and then she stomped out of the tent before she actually did lay her hands on him to throttle him round the neck. David's mouth twitched as he attempted not to smile. He remarked, "That was a cruel thing to say."

"She needed a reminder of her place." Pierre answered stiffly.

"Is it true?"

"What?"

"It's tonight."

Owen, their proper servant, interrupted them at this point "Sirs, we have to decamp.

Should I pull down the tent?"

"Who was this from?" David asked.

"Bohemond sent out his servants to tell everyone Master Renard."

"Start taking down the tent then and find Constance to help you pack." Pierre ordered. Owen had been let in on the secret to make life easier and he had also been threatened with death if even a whisper of Constance was heard from someone else's mouth.   "Yes sir."

"I'm going to find out more." David got to his feet and left the tent.

"I'm coming with you." Pierre called out as he hurried out of the tent after his brother.

With the camp completely packed up they set off east towards the mountains. The following night a few were left to guard the women, injured and supplies. The majority returned with the fall of darkness. They made for the guarded area of Antioch's many towered wall which was being held by their inside contact. A ladder had been tied against the wall between two silent towers where only a torch flickered in each but no men. Sixty soldiers scrambled up and quickly took possession of six towers. More ladders were thrown over and shouts of excitement and relief were heard as more soldiers began climbing up even as the original ones broke under the weight of armoured men climbing them.

A small gate in the wall, the Gate of St George, hidden in shadows was finally noticed and men headed for them. They pushed the wooden gate open and the rest of the army of Crusaders poured into the city and began extracting revenge for making them suffer the nine-month siege of starvation and cruel weather.

No one at the beginning was spared, neither Christians nor Muslims or Jews. Buildings were set alight and with a background of these flames Pierre killed anyone that moved, his blood thirstiness enhanced by his hunger and need to honour his God with blood of Christ's enemies. Soon religion was sorted out amongst the citizens and Christians were soon aiding the Crusaders in killing the Muslims.

Yaghi Siyan was not to be found. He had escaped. His son retreated into the citadel high on the ridgetop and decided to remain there with the few soldiers he could rally round him. He could only hope that Kerbogha was successful in ridding the city of Crusaders so he could take his father's place as ruler of Antioch. He hoped his father had gone in search of their allies and would return with them soon.

They only had enough time to rid the city of fast decaying corpses from the hot sun and decide the defence of the city before Kerbogha arrived and they ended up being trapped in Antioch instead with limited supplies and with the citadel still full of Sacrens. Word got through that the Byzantine Emperor had turned round and gone home on the word of Stephen of Blois and his opinion that the Crusaders were going to fail. Many curses were spoke on the Frenchman that day as well as on the Emperor for believing the man. Moral reached an all time low especially as Kerbogha almost captured one of the city's four hundred towers and that was only due to there being not enough Crusaders to watch over all of them.

However hungry they were the Renard brothers resisted the urge to eat their horses. Admittedly they did draw blood out of the three they had. Owen's had been taken so now the three they had left were always watched by either Owen or Constance while the brothers with another soldier guarded their tower which over looked the Saracen camp. When Constance brought them food neither brother dared ask what it was. They had already heard about the robbing of fresh graves for the bodies and that any living animal found wandering the streets alone was killed.

She watched her cousins eat as she warmed her hands before the brazier that was barely burning the night's piece of wood. The tiny flames weakly licked up the piece before vanishing beneath it again like a mouse disappearing into its hole at the sight of a predator, "There's a crazy man in our midst."

"That's nice." Pierre muttered with a full mouth.

"Claims he sees St Andrew leading him to where the Holy Lance lies in the cathedral here."

"Sounds like a coincidence to me." Pierre returned. "I've heard about this." The soldier said out loud, "It's not just this one time. He's been having them for several months, visions of St Andrew I mean, and if that's true that's enough for me. I say dig it up and with that at our side we should be able to defeat the bastards outside and inside these walls." He smiled at them, pleased with his statement. Those on the outer walls of the city were safer than those close to the citadel. Bohemond had threatened to burn the houses down as those hiding in them wouldn't venture out to fight as the citadel Sacrens kept making raids out of their safe stronghold. From the bristly-chinned soldier Constance looked to David, "What do you think?" He shrugged his shoulders.

"If they'd just dig in the place they'd soon be proven wrong I bet you." Pierre remarked.

"Your horse?" The soldier offered hopefully.

"This time it was a figure of speech. You don't need a horse anyway since you're only a foot soldier." Pierre said fiercely.

"A man can try can't he?" The soldier said brightly undaunted by Pierre, "it would make good eating."

"I'll believe it when I see it or if someone else has the same vision. Who is the man who claims to have had these visions anyway?" David asked calmly.

"A servant of Count Raymond's." Constance informed him.

"That figures." Pierre muttered harshly.

Constance glared at Pierre fiercely, annoyed that he had interrupted. Turning back to

David she finished, "He goes by the name of Peter Bartholomew."

"Definitely don't believe him then and I bet the Bishop doesn't either." Pierre said.   "A priest is safer then a servant since he's closer to God." David commented thoughtfully. "Hey! Look!" Constance pointed over the walls to the Saracen camp. The three men turned and just caught sight of a meteor falling into the siege camp which landed with a loud thump that the whole city heard and everyone turned to look down at the siege camp to see what had happened. There was movement in the camp as well as soldiers went to investigate the meteor and discuss what it meant. Constance exclaimed as she leant over the wall in the hope of seeing more, "Did you see that? What was it David?"

"A sign from God that they will die I feel."
"How?"

"By our hand." David answered without emotion, hiding the hopefulness he was suddenly feeling that maybe Pierre's overwhelming faith in God might actually win out.

"Just you two?" The soldier asked in awe.

"Don't be stupid, all of us; the whole army." Pierre answered back with a look that told the solider that Pierre thought him a fool.

"Should we go tell?" Constance enquired with eyes still wide from the event of seeing a meteor fall.

"Only if someone else doesn't tell." David answered calmly.

"We should tell." Pierre announced as he got to his feet, "Be the first to report it for once."

"Someone else had a similar vision you know and it was a priest." The soldier put in.   "We've moved on from that." Pierre said as if he still believed the soldier to be a fool, "I'm going to tell and I need someone else. They won't believe one man, David; come on. Constant stay with this fool of a man and make sure he doesn't do anything stupid."
David reluctantly followed Pierre from the tower but it seemed they weren't the only ones who had seen the meteor and wanted to be the first to report it. Seeing the group Pierre sneered and then took hold of David and led him away as he muttered, "Too late and only because of Connie and that stupid soldier."

"There's always another time. Anyway we should be on guard still and since it's quiet I'm going to have a sleep."
"Whatever." Pierre said distractedly while he continued to fume.

"Were you listening?"

"You'd have thought they would be trying to attack us off guard. It's been too quiet."
"You've heard the shouting brother as much as I have." David pointed out as they climbed the stairs, "There is discord amongst them. We should take advantage though only God knows whether our leaders are going to do so."
"Hmmm."

By now they had reached the top of the tower. Pierre crossed to the edge and looked down on the Saracen camp. For a brief moment he wished he was one of the Saracens and was able to eat something decent though he wasn't to know they were starving just like the Crusaders in the besieged city. He scowled to himself as he realised what he had been thinking. In reality what he really wanted was to be gone from Antioch and heading towards Jerusalem so the three of them could then go home. He could go home with tales to tell and be able to say he had been to the lands written of in the Bible. He growled in frustration and clenched his hands into fists before returning to the brazier where David glanced at him briefly before closing his eyes.

David wiped tiredness from his heavy eyes. Whenever he tried to sleep he failed miserably. All the worries had given him insomnia. Looking round everyone was looking tired and trying to ignore empty stomachs. For the last few days since the Holy Lance was found they had all been fasting and visiting the churches and confessing their sins ready for the fight. Many felt sure that the fireball and Holy Lance were all positive omens from God that they would win against the Sacrens.

David felt nothing as Count Raymond of Toulouse showed them the Holy Lance that had been found thirteen days ago in the Cathedral of St Peter in the city. To be honest he wasn't sure what to make of it. He looked to Pierre but he was nodding on his horse, a similar horse to David's; all skin and bone and a sorry sight at that. Looking around at everyone else only a few others were on horseback. Most were standing with armour missing links or swords and shields looking battered and slightly rusted or bloodstained. There was an atmosphere of hope and fear amongst everyone.

Count Raymond led the Crusaders out across the Orontes River and got them into formation. David and Pierre were in the third row with the rest of the Normans. Already some were beginning to perk up as blood began to run faster through their bodies and adrenalin began to wake them up.

They had lasted this long so none planned to back down now. The few horses seemed to quiver as they sensed the approaching battle. Backs were straightened and men revealed their true heights as if God had bestowed His faith directly into their souls.

An unarmed messenger ran across from Kerbogha's side but he was soon sent fleeing by Count Raymond. Down the lines of Christians the Count shouted, "They wanted a truce but we will not give them such a thing. For the faith God has in us by revealing to us the Holy Lance that harmed Christ we will kill the infidels standing before us."
It wasn't the biggest cheer that had ever happened but there was one. A loud cheer echoed off the towers and walls above the Bridge Gate from those left guarding the walls and towers of the city. Those by the citadel heard it echo off the mountain and felt stronger.. Half of the remaining population came and watched the battle from the ramparts. They were feeling almost as blood thirsty at the thought of a battle as some of the Crusaders. They shouted down from the battlements encouragement to their side and insults at the Saracens although it was soon lost by the louder sounds of battle. Stones occasionally were thrown but didn't go far.

Horses shook their heads and men rattled as swords came out. Comparing the two armours it was obvious the Crusaders would have a good chance of winning as they had more protection then the Saracens with their light leather armour.

Under a rain of arrows the Saracens began a teasing game with the Crusaders by retreating before planning to turn, surprising the other army and causing complete destruction. However they were in a tight spot with what supplies they had behind them. The Crusaders charged in and began to slaughter the enemy with strokes of their heavy double-edged swords while counter-acting return strokes with their body length shields. David fought hard, cutting himself a path through the infantry as they tried to pull him from his horse though there were moments when it felt like his horse would collapse under him and leave him to the mercy of the Saracens.

A cry rose as the fighting began to turn against them. Those on the edge of the fighting later claimed they saw a white army come down from the mountain, rising up dust but the hooves of their horses weren't touching the ground. Something was clearly seen as their enemy's strength and fight began to drain from them.

As they weakened Kerbogha's allies began to desert the man. With all his supporters gone, leaving only his men left, Kerbogha turned coward himself and fled as well. They weren't allowed to escape as the horseback Crusaders chased after them, felling many with wide swings from their swords. Pierre was one of the many that followed the fleeing Saracens shouting at them as his exhausted horse fought on at Pierre's jabbing spurs' command. The Crusaders only turned and returned to Antioch as the local Armenians appeared to inflict more damage on the fleeing Saracens.

Arriving back at the city both brothers slipped off their horses before they collapsed under their armoured riders. David bent down and shrugged his hauberk off whether it was a suitable place or not. His chest heaved equally to Pierre's. Looking at his younger brother Pierre grinned, "fleeing with tails between their hind legs like the dogs they are. We won. God was truly on our side. It's time to celebrate. Lets go see what we can find in their camp." He headed out of the city to Kerbogha's camp where a few people were already there. David remained standing just inside the gates of Antioch with the reins of both sweating horses in his hands, watching his brother head to the camp. He leant against the shoulder of his horse, trying to stay upright as he felt sure his tired body would otherwise drop.

With a sigh he turned away and picked up the hauberk and dumped it over the saddles of his horse before leading them to the tower that was their responsibility.

Pierre was an hour in returning but he had a few sweetmeats he was proud to have claimed as his. He shared them with David, Constance and Owen willingly. They savoured the sweet taste of them as they were the first decent food eaten in a long while. With a full mouth Pierre remarked, "As I was coming this way there was shouting and you won't believe who was doing it; Count Raymond and Bohemond."

"About what?" Constance asked as she wiped the back of her hand across her sticky lips. Seeing her do so David couldn't believe what a man she had turned into. "If it's not the infidels then it is us arguing and if its not us then its them." David inputted but no one dained to respond to that though they looked at him. Pierre went back to looking at Constance to answer her question, "Don't know." He shrugged his shoulders, "I wanted to get these back before they spoiled completely in this heat."

"They were beginning to." She remarked.

"That didn't stop you from eating them." He pointed out to her.

"Look." David said looking to the citadel with an upturned face. Cousin and brother looked with Pierre wiping a hand across his lips. He glanced to his brother as he asked, "What about it?"

"The banners, they have changed."

"So."

David waited a moment for the breeze to straighten the banners out as he sheltered his eyes with a hand against the evening light and setting sun, "They are Bohemond's. The infidel inside must have surrendered."

"Why to him? I thought Count Raymond was in command of the troops and our leader." Constance questioned David. "I don't know; I'm not an infidel am I?" He replied in irritation, "I don't know every answer."

"Who will claim the city as theirs?" Pierre asked. David remained looking to the citadel making Pierre go, "Davy?" "As I've just said I don't know everything. Anyway, is there any food left?" Constance handed the last sweetmeat over in the hope it would sweeten David's mood, "I hope we move on from this place soon; I'm sick of it. I just want to get to Jerusalem."

"We all do." Pierre commented straight back.

David suddenly got to his feet, "I'm going to the cathedral, anyone coming?"
"Why?" Constance enquired.
"Is there a moment when you do use your mind or don't you have one?" Pierre snapped as he got to his feet, "You know perfectly well why Davy and I are going and you are going to come with us as well." Pierre ordered her sharply. She frowned at him, annoyed he had snapped at her but said nothing as she began to sulk and drag her feet behind her cousins. Neither brother said anything though she wanted one of them to recognise the fact she was present but both seemed to be annoyed with her. She meekly followed them to the front of the church to make the sign of the cross to Christ on his cross before skirting pass the hole dug to retrieve the Holy Lance. They knelt in a corner to thank God for their continuing lives and the victory they had had against the Saracens.

Chapter 10

July 1148

It had taken them almost half a year to just get through the straits between Spain and Africa and round to Tortosa where they were now being expected to help Count Ramon Berenguer IV of Barcelona get the Moors out of the fortified city on the left bank of the Ebre River inland twelve miles. Behind the walls of the sloping hillside were granite built homes with narrow streets. Watching over them was the Zuda Castle at the hill's crest. The Pope wanted it reclaimed since it had supposedly become a haunt for pirates supported by the Moors.

The Normans with the Knight Templar set up beside a mill on the river north of the city. Most of the sailing Crusaders had carried on with the trip in the hope of finally getting to the Holy Lands but some had remained in Lisbon and a few like Turstan had returned home. Pascal was not sure what to make of the knights of the Temple who to him were a bit arrogant and snobby. They were all trained knights though they were monks as well and had made the same monastic promises as normal monks would.

Though Gallien had respect for monks and the Templar Knights he personally thought them mad to not be interested in women especially now that he had discovered them over the winter in Lisbon. He felt that some must ignore the vow and go to a brothel occasionally. He tried to follow them around out of curiosity. However he soon gave up as he was caught and asked whether he wished to become one. At that he had stuttered an answer of rejection and ran off feeling rather foolish especially as they had been preparing to pray.

Running to his father he got a slap round the ear for having vanished like that and worrying the elder Renard, "You mother would not be best pleased with me if I returned alone. What were you doing anyway?"

"Nothing."

"Liar but I won't be able to get it out of you so I won't persist. Just stop what you are doing and behave yourself before you get into trouble. You are in the territory of being a man and not a boy."

"Yes father."

"We have more sense then the Genoese who walk straight into a fight without preparation. We wait for the right moment."

"Maybe boldness is better though." A Knight of the Temple approached from behind surprising both Renards. He smiled in amusement as he added, "I apologise for I didn't mean to surprise you."

"What do you mean?" Pascal enquired.

"I'm sure the Moors have heard about the Lisbon siege before we got here. They would have been surprised and perhaps we could have won."

"We didn't though. Our ally was slaughtered." Gallien pointed out.

"An equal number of the enemy were killed and harmed." The man replied. There was a twinkle in his brown eyes, which made Gallien smile.

"I think we deserve to know your name." Pascal remarked with some suspicion.

"I suppose you deserve to know." The knighted monk held out a hand, "George after the knight who helped us win with his army of white at Ascalon."

"No army of white was seen. My grandfather was there and he didn't see anything like that." Gallien said with a frown. "Then he didn't believe." George remarked.

"Don't speak about my father like that." Pascal said with warning, still having not shaken the man's hand so George finally put it down.   "I'm sorry."

"He prayed to God everyday as any good Christian should. Go, get lost. I'm not having you insult my family." "I did not mean to."

"What do you want anyway?" Pascal demanded.

"I heard you were guarding the Bishop in Lisbon."

"Come to have a go at us then?"

"It wasn't our fault." Gallien put in nervously. He looked to his father and could see the Templar Knight was winding him up.

"I don't expect it was."

"Just go then." Pascal said while trying to remain calm.

Seeing that the atmosphere around them was becoming threatening George decided it was time he left and cheerfully said, "Maybe I'll see you around again some time." He gave the pair a wave as he headed away.

"Good riddens to bad rubbish." Pascal muttered.

"Why father?"

"Didn't like him from the moment he spoke."

The two siege towers that were ordered were rapidly built. They were two high towers of wood and animal skin set on wheels with platforms and ladders inside. The Crusaders watched as the Genoese climbed the two towers and began to break down the walls while archers kept the inhabitants of the city at bay. By the end of the day they got inside the city and went about destroying homes and tower houses up to the Mosque of the city.

A third was heeled across the wood and stone filled ravine and once through the city wall headed to the eastern wall of the citadel. The defenders had small catapults on the walls and attacked back, damaging the siege tower.
The Genoese fought hard for several months to get into the Citadel with the Crusaders looking on with bemusement. Their numbers had depleted after men who had not been paid their dues had left. Many were beginning to wonder why they had stopped at Tortosa when it looked as if they weren't needed.

The constant battering from the siege engines finally began to frighten the Moors within. Messages were sent out with an offer of surrender. A hundred Moors were sent as hostages to the Genoese while the Moors tried to seek help from their allies. With no help for the Moors after the promised forty days they surrendered reluctantly but it was easier then having the Genoese continue to slowly weakening them.

There was triumphant for the Genoese soldiers and the Count as they entered the city with their banners over the Zuda Castle. Gallien was not happy about it at all, "What was the point of us being here? All we've done is be peasants to them."

"Sssh Gallien, at least it is over."

"Can we go home now?"

"We must give our thanks to God for the victory." Pascal answered calmly, not the answer Gallien had wanted. "What victory? Look around you father. Only our ally is happy." Gallien pointed out fiercely with a wave of his arm. Pascal sighed, "I know but we must put a happy face on it all." "Do we now go home?" Gallien asked again.

"Gallien please stop asking me that question. We are not going home just yet.

Tomorrow I am going to start organising the journey to the Holy."

"Why? By the time we get there we won't be needed."

"So what. We are going." Pascal answered sternly, "this is a once in a lifetime trip to see the lands of our Lord."
Gallien frowned at his father, "what are you not telling me? I'm not a boy anymore so you can't keep treating me like one."
Pascal studied his son with his developing beard and then from his belongings he pulled out the letter his mother had given him. It was now a little crumpled but the seal was still intact.
"What is that?"

Pascal turned the letter over and over in his hands, resisting the temptation to open it. Finally he stopped, "this was given to me by my mother. Though he hasn't been spoken of much recently, as I recall, there might be a relative, an uncle, in Jerusalem.
If he lives then I am to give him this."

"What's in it?"

"I don't know. I swore never to open it."

"I thought your uncle had died at Jerusalem?"

"So did I, so did I." Pascal answered thoughtfully as he put the letter away. He wondered what it would mean for his family if he found his uncle alive. Would he find peace for his family? Whenever he had observed his mother and father they had never quite fitted together as if it had been an awkward arranged marriage. As he had grown older he wondered if there was someone missing in their relationship and perhaps it was this uncle who no one knew whether was alive or dead.

Chapter 11

Spring/early summer 1149

At the nearest sea port where there had to be trade ships that would be travelling across the Mediterranean Sea to the Holy Lands Pascal hung around questioning the captains and trying to get them to understand his French. It was through pure luck that he found anyone at all. The merchant was ready to leave with his cargo, which was heading for the Holy Lands. The man was cheerful even if neither spoke the other's language and what words they knew were poorly spoken. Admittedly it did cost Pascal some of the Lisbon loot but at least it would mean he and Gallien would rapidly get away from Spain. He was not bothered by the fact the man was a black Moor.

The man's trade boat had a high prow while at the stern of its thirty-five metre length was a flat end. The rudder stretched the whole height of the stern as well as dipping into the sea. At the stern were two cabins though they looked rather rickety as if they had been put up in haste and actually rarely used. The mast was close to the jutting up bow. The sail was rolled up while on the dockside but when down it would be revealed to be triangular. Most of the loading had been done when the two Renards had arrived and much was stowed away in the open hull and was being covered in oiled leathercloth.

When they left Pascal was glad to have the wind behind them, blowing them across the sea and to be seeing the back of Spain where the Moors still held many pockets of land. He and the Captain managed to strike up a conversation

with the other being very proud that he had two Renards, "I know of a man who goes by Renard, in fact several. He buys from me if I have a good cargo." He smiled a slightly toothy grin in his pride, "He is a good merchant, very good."
"What's his name?"

"Aaah, he goes by the name of David Renard. He is a good man. Are you family?"

"Perhaps."

"Though maybe not as he is one of us." The man scratched his forehead knocking the cloth wrapped round his head back to reveal a bald head underneath that glistened slightly in the sun from the beads of sweat there. He had a grisly white beard on his chin and a weather beaten face.

"A Mohammed?" It was another piece of the puzzle but none as yet seemed to fit together. Pascal frowned but the Capitan appeared not to be bothered as he slapped Pascal on the back, "Come, have a drink with me."

"He can't be a Mohammed father." Gallien remarked, "He can't be if he's grandfather's brother."
"You listening in, you make a good spy." The Captain beamed revealing his white teeth again, "drink with me also." He led the way into the cabin still smiling and found a bottle of wine for them to share. It appeared he wasn't bothered by the rules of religion.

It wasn't long before Gallien began to feel sick again and he left to sit against the mast and occasionally run to the side to throw up over it. The Captain could only chuckle, "He won't make a good sailor."
Pascal sighed, "I think we'll be returning home overland."

"That's more dangerous then the sea."

"I don't think so."

"Bandits, murderers. I have heard about them all from my brother and he a good truthful man."

"You have pirates though." Pascal pointed out.

"They no trouble."

"Hmmm." Pascal turned from the Captain where they stood just outside the cabin looking across to Gallien and looked out to sea and the vanishing land mass that was Spain with its fighting Moors and Christians, "so what is this Renard like?"

"An old man now. I remember when we first met." The captain beamed, pleased to have an audience for one of his stories, "he plays good chess. He lives in Jerusalem and sells to those infidels." The captain spat out the word and Pascal had to guess that he meant the Christians who had reclaimed Jerusalem in the last crusade, "they just take and take. They don't look after anything they buy. They have no respect for anything but David, he has lots. It is said that he has many children and they are well known as well. He has buried a wife and his trading partner but he goes on as if he is waiting for something, that's what his grandson tells me."

"Waiting for something?"

"Only Allah knows, maybe it is you." The captain suggested loving the mystery of it all.

"Has it been said that he had a brother or where he came from?"

"Not that I know of but he was drawn to Allah by his love, his first wife. I have seen her. She was one beauty. I would happily have taken her to my bed." The captain winked with a knowledge that left Gallien blushing.

"Oh." Pascal felt slightly disappointed that it wasn't going to be solved there and then. It might still be that this David Renard was someone else's uncle and not his

□

He was pleased they had found a ship to get them to St Symeon, the closest port to Antioch. Around the port town the landscape was coarse green shrubbery mixed with trees of citrus fruits and corn as well as herds of sheep and goats. Vineyards lined some of the slopes along with farms and their fields. Gallien was thankful that the voyage was over but wasn't pleased to be even further away from home and into unknown territory even if it was where the Son of God had lived.

Pascal wanted to get to Jerusalem as quick as possible now. He hoped maybe to be a Crusader in the Holy Lands but word was soon found that many had gone home and it was over. Gallien looked to his father when they heard that news from the Moorish Captain who had been speaking with others and asked, "Where do we go now? What do we do?" "We still go to Jerusalem."

"How do we get there?"

"I'll buy us some horses and we'll get there for we have the money." He looked at his now nineteen-year-old son. "If you wait David Renard will appear." The Captain remarked behind them, surprising them both, "He should be here soon to look at my goods. It maybe his son or grandson though but I hope it is him for we have good conversations together."

"I'd rather not." Pascal said with a frown.

"That's a great pity. I hope you find your uncle, maybe it will be him."

"Thank you." Pascal returned thoughtfully for if the man mentioned by the sailor was really his uncle he would have cousins and from their children as well.

The two related men actually passed each other without even knowing they did. The Moorish Captain greeted

Mansur with a smile, "Have you come to buy my goods?" He gestured around while remaining seated on the stone the ship was tied to. His crew was still unloading his cargo but that didn't seem to matter to him.

"Not this time." Mansur, named after his great grandfather, replied with a soft smile compared to the Captain's white beam. He had merely been doing a last minute stroll along the quays before organising the return trip to Jerusalem.

"Why are you here then? How is your grandfather?"

"He is as well as ever. I actually think my father wishes he would die sometimes so that he can take over. My grandfather just won't hand over the reins."

"Do not say such things Mansur or Allah may strike you down… Aaah, that has just reminded me."
"Reminded you?"

"Yes. I had two passengers by the name of Renard."

"I know my grandfather has a brother."

"So he could be related. He's gone in search of horses to make his way to Jerusalem. He's after a man by your grandfather's name so he might be the one he is after. He was certainly fascinated with what I knew."

"Which direction did he go in?" Mansur asked, intrigued by the Captain's passengers now. He never thought he might have a cousin from his grandfather's brother.

"They; there were two of them, father and son."

"I'll go find them for I'm sure they won't know what way to go." Mansur headed off.

"Hey!" The Captain got to his feet, "What about my goods?"

Mansur turned, "I told you I wasn't buying. I only came down to see if you were here."

"What am I suppose to do then?" The Moor exclaimed, "I was hoping you would take some of it. I didn't have to come here you know."

"But you did. I'm sure others will want what you've got."

"Hmpfh." The Moor crossed his arms and dropped back on to the quayside stone and muttered in annoyance, "Not if they know Renard rejected my goods." He had been hoping to sell at least half his goods to the Renards. The Moor scowled as another trader appeared to see what he had that was worth buying. He now knew he wasn't going to get the best price and that there would be some hard bargaining about to happen as the trader would have noticed Mansur leaving without anything.

"Maybe later." Mansur called back as he vanished through the docks' crowds. Mansur hurried through the streets with little clue of what the two men he was looking for looked like in appearance. He could only guess that they would look out of place and would be struggling with the language. Ahead of him he caught sight of two men dressed in chain mail and obviously not soldiers on duty as they held no spears. Staring around, pausing to let others past while clearly trying to work out what to do. He shouted in the French his grandfather had taught him, "hey! Stop! Wait!" The two men turned with Pascal frowning as he saw the young man who was slightly older than his son run up to him. His skin was tanned from the sun and his brown hair had sun bleached streaks in it. He questioned, "Who are you? What do you want? How come you speak my language?"

"You are looking for David Renard?" Mansur enquired in French with a heavy accent. He was mildly surprised that the man he now stood before looked similar to his grandfather when the elderly man had been younger.
Pascal became hopeful, "Yes. Where can I find him?"

"He is my grandfather. Why do you not join me on my return journey to Jerusalem?

It would be cheaper then buying yourselves horses for I have enough animals." "I don't know." Pascal became suspicious and eyed the young man up who was by now smiling, thinking he had found himself another family relation.
"I wish to cause you no harm."

"How do I know you are speaking the truth?"
"Look at me, do you think I would speak your language normally?"

"If you are a trader then you could easily learn the language."

"Why don't you at least travel with me to get to Jerusalem?" Mansur suggested, still with a friendly smile on his brown face, "Do you know the way?"
"That I don't so I suppose I could join you, thank you."

"Come eat with me then. We'll depart tomorrow." "What about horses?" Gallien enquired.
"Do not worry. I have enough animals." Mansur turned to look at Gallien.

"Don't you have trading to do?"

"I did most of it yesterday." Mansur answered, "Now will you let me buy you something to eat for I'm sure you are hungry."
"Thank you." Pascal answered before his son could ask any more questions.

With the morning Pascal and Gallien stared at the train of laden camels and horses with a few servants checking ropes on the animals and load. Mansur was proud of the family's beasts and remarked, "They are all good. Which do you wish to ride?"

"How long is the journey?" Pascal asked as he eyed the sliding jaw of a kneeling camel. Behind its long eyelashes it looked straight back at him before its head was pulled round by Mansur to loosen the taut rope to untie it. Over the camel's head Mansur answered, "about a week but it depends how well we do each day and if we don't get attacked by bandits."

"Bandits?"

"Don't worry I am armed and you two should be as well."
"With what?"

"I have my grandfather's sword, the one he takes and the one my father takes when we travel." Mansur replied with confidence. He pulled the sword from its worn scabbard which was attached to the saddle on the camel he was to be riding. He showed it to them with pride and the iron glinted in the bright sunlight. Pascal stared in astonishment for it looked the same as his father's especially with the fanciful dragon etched into the top of the blade. He wondered momentarily if it had been stolen but looking at Mansur's honest beaming face of pride he decided that it couldn't be so as Mansur showed it willingly to the two crusaders. Mansur added, "And you have your swords as well." He pointed to them at the Normans' sides, "So, come on, camel or horse?"

"What are you going to be riding?"

"Camel." Mansur answered with a smile, "They are good to ride if you are use to their walk and get the right position."
"I think I'll take a horse." Pascal decided.

Gallien frowned for a moment and then followed his father's decision. Mansur remarked, "As you wish. There are two with no loads, take these blankets for they aren't saddled."
At that moment the camel became the most welcoming option

but David thought it best not to change his mind at the beginning of a tentative friendship. He took the blankets and threw them over the two horses' backs while Mansur roped the other good laden horses and his two camels together. The two Normans got up on their horses while Mansur pulled himself on to his camel and rapped its rump with a stick and tugged at its rope reins to get the humped beast to stand. It stood with a lot of complaining surprising Pascal and Gallien especially when Mansur said in Arabic,

"Stop your complaining, you've up now."

Chapter 12

August 1149

While Mansur's servants and some of his cousins unloaded the Normans looked up at the walls of Jerusalem and the gold cross that stood above the Muslims' Dome of the Rock Mosque. The walls still looked battered from the attack during the First Crusade. There was no sound of the Muslim call to pray which David and Pierre had heard when They had reached Jerusalem. Instead Pascal and Gallien heard bells ring for evening mass from several churches within the city. Mansur paused and looked at the two men, "What are you going to do now?"
Pascal looked to the Arab, "Well… I might try your grandfather if you don't mind. Is this really Jerusalem?"
"That it is, my home and its peaceful now that the Crusaders have gone. My grandfather will enjoy seeing you if you are really related to us. It is his birthday today."

"Then perhaps I shouldn't intrude." Pascal returned cautiously.

"No, no. He won't mind. He welcomes everyone. And if he's not the man you are looking for he will still be able to help. He knows everyone here in Jerusalem and will be able to point you in the right direction."
"But he doesn't know us."

"That doesn't matter." Mansur smiled, "He knows whether you are worth welcoming by the look of you. Come on and I will take you there."

"What about…?" Pascal gestured to Mansur's family members and servants.

"They can look after it all. So, are you coming?"

"Sure." Pascal finally said. Mansur was already heading towards the gate and he had to catch up with him and Gallien who was eager for a proper bed and food.

Mansur pushed his way through the narrow streets confidently while Pascal and Gallien trailed behind. There was the smell of intoxicating spices, which seemed to almost rise up in clouds from the heat. There was also the sound of men and boys at work hammering at brass, working with wood and leather as well as shouting about their wares. As well as that there was the making of carpets with shuttles going from right to left and back on the looms. All the workshops appeared to be mixed up in the arrivals' eyes but only because they were trying to take it all in. Each street contained one industry from the cobblers up to the selling of fruit and vegetables and spices.

There was no peace at all and it all crowded the visitors' senses. They couldn't stop their eyes shifting from right to left to take in all the bright colours and patterns especially against the white painted buildings. It made life in England in the country look pretty dull in Gallien's opinion.

At one point the two halves of the small party lost each other in the streets. Mansur, realising he had lost the others, stopped and tried to look over the tops of people to find them. He smiled with relief as he caught sight of their shuffling bodies. He always loved observing new visitors to Jerusalem. Yes he was a follower of Mohammed but he could still understand the awe and bewilderment of the city where three religions swung between peaceful co-habitation and anger.

Finally they reached the house. The sound of a lute could be heard through the lattice-decorated gates. Pascal and

Gallien paused outside the gates as Mansur headed in. Pascal was feeling nervous but then decided he was actually terrified. His heart was beating hard in his ribcage and he didn't think he could actually enter a stranger's home even if it was possibly his uncle. Was he about to ruin someone's celebrations?

Mansur looked to Pascal with a hand on the gate and so did Gallien. Mansur enquired,

"Is everything all right?"

 "Lets do this." Pascal answered stiffly.

Mansur smiled and pushed open the gate and gestured Pascal and Gallien to go in before him. As Pascal stepped in he thought of a question but it was too late to ask it for he became astonished by the sight of the fountain and the green potted plants and the Jasmine covered house.

Never had he seen so many people crammed into one house. Not even Christmas dinner with the villagers at the manor had looked so crowded. Amongst the green plants children ran about, playing and chasing cats. The women were gathered on one side talking amongst themselves as they prepared the feast to celebrate their father and father-in-law's birthday. Their father's birthday was always a good reason for the whole family to be brought together to catch up on births, deaths and other family gossip. The men sat opposite talking business. The one person they were all staying clear of sat on cushions with a grey-haired woman, Sir David Renard. Pascal sensed a power that needed to be respected coming from the old man. There was also authority, more than his father ever had.

The elderly David had heard the gates of his home open and looked to the lute player, his youngest son, who stopped playing almost instantly. David turned his brown aged face to the visitors and demanded in Arabic, "Who are you? Come closer so I can see you. My sight isn't as good as it use to be."

Mansur told his father, "They do not know the language father."

In French with a hint of an Arabic accent David said, "Come closer and tell me who you are."

Pascal felt he had to obey out of respect. The words had been spoken with authority but it was a gentle one in tone as if the man never abused his power as head of a large family and creator of a thriving business. He approached the man, "Are you Sir David Renard?"

"That I am but who are you?" David repeated with sternly.

"My name is Pascal Renard sir and this is my son Gallien." Pascal bowed his head at the elderly man.

David's eyes widened and with a shaking voice asked, "And your parents?"

David frowned, wondering why the question was being asked but he answered, "Sir

Pierre Renard and Lady Constance sir."

David gulped and then gave an order to no one in particular but one he wanted obeyed, "Someone get them some hot water and clean clothes. Get them out of those hauberks. This isn't the climate to be wearing such things."

Mansur obliged and led them up the stairs and a woman brought up a jug of hot water for them. Hadiya watched him go and felt sure she had seen something of her husband when he had been younger in the elder of the two men. There was the dirty blonde hair to start off with and a sense of a heavy build like her husband.

When Pascal re-appeared David beckoned him forward and looked him over before enquiring, "What are you doing here? You can't have come with the Crusade for they've come and gone and were unsuccessful." "We were coming round by ship sir and we ended up rescuing the city of Lisbon and

Tortosa from Moors."

"Moors?"

"Black Muslims sir…"

"Like Captain Abdul father." Mansur interrupted.
"Aaah." David said in understanding.

"Are you really my father's brother?" He felt some disbelief that he had actually found his uncle and the man really was his uncle.
David smiled, "I am."

"If you are then my mother told me to tell you that you are more important to me then I could ever imagine."
David froze and looked at Pascal again; was that his hair of his youth? He didn't really know since he didn't exactly study himself as he shaved in the metal surface that was his mirror. He looked to Hadiya and asked her in Arabic, "Do you see any of me in him?"
She cautiously nodded and asked, "Why?"

"I will explain later. Someone help me up?"

There was stiffness in his body when Pascal helped the man who he believed to be his uncle to his feet. Once on his feet David said, "Come with me Pascal." Together they entered the house's sitting room that showed evidence of regularly being used by the large family with worn furniture and cushions with impressions from being sat on by numerous bottoms. Once in there Pascal said cautiously, "My mother…"

"So she rules the home then." David smiled as he sat down.

"Err… I suppose so."

"I did not meant to interrupt but how is she? Do the pair of them still argue? Do you have any siblings?" "My mother is well but my father is dead."

"Oh," David looked glum then, "Since when?"

"Four years back now."
"And are you the eldest?"

"I am the only one though I am married with a son and a daughter. But what has happened to the Crusaders? They were meant to be rescuing Jerusalem but no one is here and it doesn't feel like it needs saving."
David just looked at Pascal for a moment before answering the question.

He had been relieved back in July when the Franks had left Jerusalem for Damascus. Yes, he had made plenty of passing business but the whole city had been chaotic and unsafe. With so many crusaders filling the streets bursting for a fight with anyone who wasn't Christian or didn't look like Christians David had given orders for his whole family to remain behind the gates of their home. Only he and his eldest walked the streets as they were trusted by the old crusaders from the Crusade he had arrived with though even then they both carried knives for protection. He had never sold so much wine in his whole trading life. That had been due to the new advocate of Jerusalem entertaining the king and queen of France as well as Raymond of Toulouse who had control of Antioch.

Finally David answered Pascal, "They left a month back. They came to

Jerusalem and found it at peace."

"What do you mean?" Pascal asked with disappointment.

"Did you not notice that peace reigns in this city. They came expecting a battle and found that there was none to have.

They went on to Damascus to satisfy their thirst for innocence blood. I feel they will return home empty handed as they do not have enough men. It is said that they lost a lot of men on the way down as well as many becoming demoralised since they were forced by the queen to remain in Antioch for a long time."

"Oh… then we have been lied to." Pascal remarked.

"It happens. Come though there is family to be introduced to. That boy, is he your son?"

"Gallien, yes." Pascal replied uncertainly. He was still feeling shocked that he had missed the Holy Land Crusade though nothing had happened. There was also the fact he had somehow stumbled into a giant family of Renards where the patriarch was willingly accepting him as a part of it from his motherland. He decided to wait a few days before giving this David Renard the letter his mother had given him.

June 1099

After almost a year long delay so they weren't camped outside Jerusalem during the dry season the Crusaders set up camp around the north and west walls of Jerusalem. The Normans were camped at the north walls. It had been a long year of surviving both sieges, restless grumpy leaders and a lack of food. The Renards were glad to have finally reached Jerusalem.

Having reached the city brothers and cousin looked up to the thick high walls with Pierre remarking, "We are feet away from being inside the city you realise." "First you've got to get pass those walls; watch out for that arrow." Constance exclaimed at the end. She pulled David out of the way.

"They don't like you do they?" Pierre smiled at his brother.

"Arrows are just attracted to me." David remarked as he turned away, "they have those walls but what we have to worry about at the moment is lack of water and all these people." He had to elbow a Christian out of the way as they passed through the pleading expelled Christians. The Egyptians who held the Holy City had expelled all the Christians of Jerusalem, "They've poisoned the wells as you know."

"Are we really going to just sit and wait again?" She moaned.

"Suppose so." Pierre shrugged his shoulders for he truly didn't know.

It was a few days later when Constance hurried into the tent with excitement while the brothers were cleaning their equipment. They wanted to enter the city with their armour shining to make the family name hopefully remembered forever for the sun reflecting off them. They also wanted to feel they deserved to be entering Jerusalem so it needed to be clean with no evidence of past killings. They looked up as Constance entered. She dropped to the floor, "We may have lost Peter Bartholomew but someone else has taken his place."

"That's nice." Pierre answered emotionlessly since he didn't really care.

"I won't tell you then." She replied in annoyance.

To just keep the peace David interrupted, "as you are dying to tell, tell me." She smiled at him, "Another like him wants us to attempt an assault on the city. He's convinced that God won't let us fail."

The two brothers looked to each other before David asked, "and who is this man then?"

"Don't know. A name didn't come up as we discussed it."

"And who is 'we'?" Pierre questioned with suspicion.

"The women." She answered easily before asking, "What do you think then?"

"Don't know." Both men said and David frowned as he found another loose link in his chain mail. He asked Constance, "Do you know whether the blacksmith is up and running?"

"I think he is."

"Good. Long-shanks, I might be an hour or two." David said as he got to his feet with his chain mail legging.

"There's plenty of hours in the day so take your time. I might easily be joining you anyway." Pierre replied to his hauberk and then briefly glanced up at his younger brother.

The Crusaders' generals were persuaded by the man's belief in his vision and an attack was planned. Some men were a bit uncertain about it all since the possible areas to attack were limited as well as they didn't have the right equipment to attack the walled city. There appeared to be a randomness to the assault as some went for the gates while others put up tall ladders against the walls to climb them. It became obvious almost immediately that the Crusaders would never get into Jerusalem however hard they tried that day. No one seemed capable of shouting the order to stop the madness as knights and infantry were pushing themselves onwards in the hope they would really get in. Men fell from ladders with arrows in their bodies or if they got close to the top of the wall slashes from sabres. Hot oil and water was poured down on them scalding many. There was no way of getting through the onslaught from the enemy.

As the day lost its light to the evening they staggered away leaving the many dead at the foot of the city's walls for the time being. They walked away like dogs with tails between their legs. Cheers and insults followed them from the walls.

Later, as they collected their dead, there was no let up as stones were thrown at them by children who should have been in bed but who had slipped out without their parents noticing. The leaders took it as a lesson that siege engines were truly needed.

Though the brothers were exhausted they couldn't fall asleep. Every time David shut his eyes he saw all the wasted lives and he felt like killing the man who had had the 'vision' and persuaded their leaders it would be good to attack. For a moment he wondered whether a too eager leader had set up the man but he quickly shook such a thought away. He felt that even their leaders were more sensible then that even if it wasn't there all the time. Pierre was the one who spoke into the darkness, "That was a wasted day you know. That got us no closer to getting into the city."

"I know. Men needlessly died today."

"What will be next I wonder?"

"Only God knows."

"I'm sick of sitting round waiting."

"They are probably planning something at this very moment for all we know. We should try to sleep." David turned on to his side from his back and rested his head on his hands. He heard his brother sigh and felt the blanket being drawn over his body as Pierre turned on to his side so both had their backs to each other. David stared into the darkness for a moment longer before closing his eyes. Outside in other tents he heard the moans of those in pain from their injuries and was glad he had missed that happening to him. On the other hand both he and Pierre were covered in bruises old and new.

Chapter 13

July 1099

It was the last evening of the fast that had been ordered by a priest who had had a vision of Bishop Adhemar. It seemed they would never get into Jerusalem until all soldiers and non-combatants had been cleansed of their sins. Pierre was not at all happy with people having more visions and even making them fast, "There was no need to starve us since we are anyway. Mother's not going to recognise either of us by the time we get home. We'll have grey hair before we are old and will be nothing but skin and bone. I'm sick of these visions; why can't they just let us get on with it and attack in our own time when we are ready; I mean that last one."

"All right Pierre." David said with warning, "That's enough. You aren't meant to be making more sins for yourself."
"Let's leave this blundering lot and go home." Pierre said impulsively.

"We are doing no such thing. We have the siege towers so we will be fine. We'll do it in the next few days once this damn fast is over."
Pierre smiled, "See, you don't like it any better then I do."

"Go away Long-shanks." David pushed his brother but was also smiling. Sobering up he added, "It ends today anyway so there really wasn't any need for you to moan. You could have done it every other day."

"What happens tomorrow then? Start a new one?" Pierre sneered.

"They've been planning something but I don't know what. We will probably get told sometime this evening."

"I hope there will be something worth eating tonight."

"That's if we eat at all."

With the new day knights put on their clean armour. Many had occupied themselves with the task while waiting for the fast to end and wanting to stop themselves from thinking about eating. They could have left it to their servants to do but none had wanted to. They felt that just this once they should do it themselves just as Pierre and David had. Over the top they put on their white surcoats with red crosses; the design that they all had adopted by now. As well as that all had white hoods attached to the cloaks they wore. Although by this time they were more yellow then white from the dust.

The army walked round the city in procession while singing psalms and with the priests leading them, swinging incense before them and carried sacred relics that had been picked up along the way. The armour reflected the sunlight and was almost dazzling especially with the pale yellow land around them. From above, on Jerusalem's walls, the Egyptians mocked them, jeered at them, "You'll never get in!

Go home! What did your Christ do for you? He lets you die!"

"I just want to kill them, cut out their tongues." Pierre hissed from the side of his mouth to David.

"Sssh." David returned and then grimaced as his bare feet stepped on a sharp stone.

"Listen to them."

"Ignore them Pierre. Sometimes I think I'm the elder since you say some stupid things." David whispered.

"Sssh." A knight behind them hissed fiercely.

After their circuit around the city they gathered on the Mount of Olives. Many stood while some men joined women and children sitting on the ground. Standing on a large boulder Peter the Hermit gave them a sermon. Count Raymond followed with his own words, "With ourselves now clean of past sins God will let us enter his great city and let us rescue it from those pigs who destroy the holiness it holds for us. We will succeed because we have God on our side. We will drive the Mohammeds and the Jews away from the city and make it safe for our people who wish to make a pilgrimage here. With Jerusalem safe we will have done what we had set out to do and we will go to Heaven at our deaths.

Our siege towers are ready and in a few days we will attack and will claim victory over the infidels who hold our Holy City captive. Each and every one of you will feel pride once we control the city as God wants us to. Our hearts will swell up with the honour of ridding the Holy City of the demons that hold it. We will win if the belief that we will and if you carry God in your hearts for we have come this far and we will not be stopped at this last obstacle. We are Normans and nothing will stop us getting what we want." He held up the Holy Lance high and the sunlight reflected off some of its exposed metal and a cheer went up. Pierre looked to his brother where
they both sat on the ground and grinned, "We will do it." He frowned then, "What are you doing?"

"Making sure I will be able to walk. There's a thorn in my foot somewhere and I'm trying to find it."

"Ignore the pain; this is more important. You should be thinking of God not your body. Our body is the vessel of our soul and to keep that pure we must think only of God until we attack."

"I heard that as well you know." David replied as he frowned in concentration. He had found the small thorn and was now trying to get it out with two fingers. He didn't want to have to use the tip of his knife to get it out and make a mess of it so he wouldn't be able to ride as well as walk. "Leave it for now. Look, Arnulf Malecome is going to speak. You've got all day to find it."

"It's a nagging pain and I've found it."

"Give it here." Pierre said in annoyance. He took David's foot and finding the thorn drew it out between two fingernails, "There you go."

"Thank you."

"Now shut up and listen." Pierre snapped as he threw the thorn away from him,

"You are so weak sometimes."

"I'm sorry." David replied feeling annoyed himself and shifted his position so he didn't have to look at Pierre.

As they returned back to their tent Constance realised that something had happened between the two brothers. Others were discussing what had been said but Pierre and David weren't. She stepped up between them and with concern asked,

"What has happened between you two?"

"That is none of your concern." Pierre returned sharply.

"I think it is because I have to live with you two until we get back to England. I'd prefer you smiling about something you've done or said connected to me then this silence. How on earth could you have argued during this morning?"

"Quite easily but as I've already said, this doesn't need you getting involved." Pierre replied harshly.

She looked hurt and hung back a moment to let them go on without her. Never had she seen the brothers argue and not make up minutes later for ease of living with the other. She hoped they would not let whatever they had argued about get between them for the rest of their lives.

If she knew what it had been about she would only be able to laugh at the insanity of it but for the brothers it had become one squabble too many on their travels to Jerusalem. Throughout the journey Pierre had always been the more passionate brother and to have David fussing over a thorn had been the last straw. He felt that David was showing disrespect for the whole Crusade by ignoring the sermon and not preparing himself religiously for the attack and grand entry into Jerusalem.

David left his brother pretending to sleep so as not to have to talk to him. He was feeling thirsty and went off to the women's side of the camp where many had gathered as their men had sent them away so as not to be tempted or tainted by sex before entering Jerusalem. He found Constance wrapped in a blanket by one of the fires talking to a group of women some of the soldiers had attracted along the way. He slipped in beside her and reached for the earthenware jug filled with some rough wine, "What we talking about?"

"Nothing much. Half of us can't sleep for worrying for tomorrow." Someone remarked from across the fire, "shouldn't you be asleep? It's going to be a long day tomorrow."

"Can't sleep. Constance can we go somewhere else?" "Of course, why?" She asked with a frown.

"No offence ladies but I don't really know any of you."

"Make sure he keeps his hands to himself." Another woman commented with a wink at Constance that made her blush. "Don't worry, he's safe." Constance responded as she got up and pulled the blanket closer around her, "What's wrong?"

"Nothing, well… Constance?" He began as they wandered off.

"Yes?" She looked up into his face as they stopped some distance away from the women. Her face felt flushed from the wine and her eyes were wide.

"I just want to apologise for Pierre."

"Why are you doing it?"

"Because he is too proud to."

"Davy, can I confess something?"

"What?"

She looked to her feet and then back up at David's puzzled face. It was then, a tipsy impulse; that caused her to reach up and kiss him firmly on the lips.

He didn't find himself pulling away, instead responding to her tentative tongue. Constance was having to rely on what she had seen and been told by other women. David took her head in his large hands. Finally she broke away to grab a breath and he asked, "What was that for?" She didn't answer, just led him further away from the women and the small flames of the fire. She stopped in a shallow dip in the ground causing David to bump into her back. She turned and pressed her lips to his again. His hands ran down her body and under the hose she still wore and he pulled her closer.

Before long they were on Constance's blanket with clothes half on and off and other parts just bunched up and out of their hands' way. Animal instincts had taken over and before either knew what was happening David was on top of Constance. There was no stopping him as he thrust into Constance, even when she cried out from the pain of her losing her virginity. As he spent himself they both came round to what had happened.

Though both were still breathing heavily from the sex

Constance, with embarrassment, adjusted all her clothes as David wiped her virgin's blood from his now limp penis. He muttered, "May the lord forgive me for what I have done."
"David." Constance whimpered, "what have we done? What if Pierre finds out? I'm going to hell!" She pulled the bloodstained blanket around her body.

"As long as you don't become with child no one will know."

"But what about when I marry?"

"How can you worry about that at a time like this?" He suddenly demanded as he still felt shocked by what had just happened. He got up and walked away. He had been foolish especially on the eve of an important battle. Constance stared in disbelief as he left, "where are you going?! Don't leave me."
David turned back to her, "I… not now Constance. I have to go."

"What about me?!" She demanded, "You did this."

"Me?!" He exclaimed, "You started this. I'm going. I can only hope that God can forgive me. You'd best pray he forgives you too. I have to go to sleep otherwise I'll be no good for anything tomorrow." He walked away and left Constance sitting there staring after him still. She was angry with herself and with David for abandoning her. He hadn't tried to restrain himself and she hadn't tried to stop him. She closed her eyes and began to pray to God to forgive her foolishness and to hope that no child had been created from the event.

The brothers were still not talking to each other when the assault on Jerusalem began with two of the siege towers up against the walls. In the night that had just gone Robert Curthose and Godfrey had got their men in position within their tower against an apparently undefended part of the walls. Pierre was in the tower since his horse had given up its life finally. David's was on its last legs and he was within the dwindling number of horseback knights. Pierre was going to be in the heart of the fighting but David, for the moment, didn't care. Only brief words had been exchanged before they went their separate ways with Pierre saying stiffly, "Don't forget our pact."

"Wasn't planning to. Where should we meet?"

"Here." Pierre answered and then turned to leave.

"Long-shanks?" David called out in a more willing voice. Pierre turned round and looked stonily at his brother, "What?"

"Good luck. You are a good soldier so I'm sure you will live."

David was willing to make up but Pierre wasn't and he gruffly replied, "You too."

Pierre jumped right into the fighting from the tower. It seemed they would never get anywhere for most of the morning but over time the Egyptians began to tire and weaknesses began to appear in their defence. Finally, after many deaths on both sides, a bridge was made across from the tower to the wall. Two Flemish knights ran across to make space on the walkway against the wall. Godfrey was not far behind to take charge of the fighting on the walls while Robert Curthose remained in the tower organising the troops in there. Pierre was sent over with his sword in hand to help in securing enough of the wall for Tancred to put his ladders against the wall. He was ready to kill all Muslims and attacked them with relish revealing a very bloodthirsty side. He barred the enemy from Tancred's ladders while soldiers scrambled up them, slashing at them with his sword and watching them bounce off his shield and fall from the wall. Godfrey's back was turned so didn't see the approaching threat of an Egyptian. Pierre saw the enemy and swung his sword at the man taking out half his neck. The Egyptian fell into the city, dead. Having felt the stirring of the air from the swing Godfrey turned, "Are you trying to kill me?"

"No sir, someone was creeping up on you. I've just killed him."

Godfrey looked slightly relieved and then with a smile said, "Come with me. We need to let the others through the gate." He beckoned with a hand and then hurried along the walkway with Pierre attempting to keep up with him while trying not to get killed in small skirmishes between enemy and comrades.

Between them they fought their way down the steps of the walkway and then through the narrow street towards the Gate of the Column. By now the streets were crowded with men from both sides fighting hand to hand combat and fighting for room to swing their swords. From above stones and pots were being thrown by feisty women determined to defend their homes from the invaders Pierre kept the enemy back until called to help open the gates. The gates swung outwards and looking out Pierre saw the last of the mounted knights as well as more infantry. Both he and Godfrey of Bouillon stood out of the way as the others entered the city. As David passed his brother he gave him a tight smile but Pierre only scowled. The soldiers piled into the city to kill the enemy who had held Jerusalem captive.

The fighting went on into the night but when Muslim soldiers were no longer to be found they moved on to civilians; anyone who was an enemy to the Christians. The Jews were killed for having been involved in getting Christ killed and the Muslims for having stopped Christian pilgrims from entering the city. As the rampage went on however even Christians lost their lives. Fires burnt in the city especially after the city's synagogue was set alight while filled with Jews who had taken refuge there.

Pierre in his zeal for bloodshed and death to all who did not believe that Jesus was the son of God was one of those brandishing a flaming stake. He crowded in with other soldiers and stopped for a moment at the sight of the cowering women and children hiding in the synagogue. More men from outside were pushing in to see what gold and riches they could grab from the Jewish Temple. Pierre was pushed aside roughly and the burning torch he held brushed against a hanging cloth. Seeing what he had done others followed suit with cries of "death to Jesus' murderers." By the time Pierre forced his way back out with tears running down his dusty face he had had enough of killing. Inside the innocent were being slaughtered with smoke billowing all around.

The Muslims who had taken shelter in the Dome of the Rock hoped Tancred who had taken the place would be kind to them and keep them safe but they weren't. Knights entered and slaughtered them as they pleaded for their lives. Some found luck on their side and were taken captive instead of killed. This didn't mean they worried any less though as they didn't know what would happen to them in the hands of the Crusaders.

Chapter 14

After a day and night of being apart Pierre headed over to the tent he was sharing with his brother in the hope of finding David already there. He had had enough of shedding innocence blood of citizens and he wondered whether he would be able to look David in the eye on the matter. He glanced at himself and couldn't believe how much blood and sooty smoke he was covered in. He dropped to the ground to wait.

For the first few hours he was patient but then he began to worry which turned into panic. As he began to search for his brother in the camp he became angry as he felt tears forming. He didn't want to return home without him. It appeared that the pact had been broken and his promise to his mother to bring David home as well. There had also always been the idea of big brother looking after little brother as he had always known his mother feared for David since he had been born small. Their mother could only ever see David as the small boy most of the time and so worried for him more than Pierre.

In the hope he might get a reply he began to shout, "Davy? Where are you?" Reluctantly he returned to their tents muttering, "you bastard, don't do this to me. Look, I'm sorry about the argument, I'm really sorry we didn't make up yesterday.

All I want is to see you again."

He sat down once back at their tent and buried his head in his hands in his misery. He jumped as he felt a hand on his shoulder. He looked up hopefully but felt only annoyance at seeing Constance looking down at him with concern. She said, "I heard someone shout for Davy and thought it might be you. Where is he then?"

"I don't know Connie."

Seeing how worked up he was she decided not to correct him on the name thing. His eyes were frantically moving all over the place and he kept turning his head. He rubbed at his arm turning it red and then also at his right calf. She asked cautiously,
"he hasn't appeared has he? You know why, it's because of that argument."

"You are wrong there." He looked behind him again pleading with God in his mind to let David appear. Someone did and hopefully he leant forwards then intuition told him it wasn't David and he seemed to shrink into himself, "we agreed to meet here."

"Give him a chance."

"I have been waiting since this morning so, no, I won't give him a chance. He's had long enough." Pierre snapped at her while continuing to be jumpy.

"That could only mean…"

"Don't say it." He warned here, "it can't be true. We promised to both live. I promised mother we would both return home. He is not dead."

"But that's the only…"

"No!" Pierre stamped his foot, "He wouldn't get himself killed, he's not stupid. He will be found. Maybe he's injured and just hasn't made it back yet." He was not going to admit that David was dead until he saw his brother's body especially as there was no sense of him being dead inside him. Only if he found David would he know whether to ignore the feeling or not.

"We can't go looking now; they are still fighting in the city. They are killing everyone Pierre and no one's stopping them."

"We have been waiting for this moment Connie. We've sat through so many sieges and any pent up emotion and energy has been released here. It can't be helped." Pierre sighed and decided not to tell her of his involvement in the burning down of the synagogue, which already he was beginning to hate himself for doing. He rubbed at his arm which was now hurting and Constance spotted it, "Are you hurt?"

"Not that I know of." He pulled off his shirt and saw no wound though it was red from his rubbing. He looked at Constance with fear, "what is wrong with me? God must be punishing me... but he can't be for I am doing his work? It must be witchcraft. One of those heathens must have put a curse on me."

Constance looked at him through wide eyes, "We need a priest."

Panic turned to common sense, "I'll be fine. Maybe I just have tired muscles."

Pierre looked grim as he watched the bodies of the many dead being taken from the blood stained streets of Jerusalem. He kept hoping that David would suddenly appear at his side and not be among the dead. After an hour he got tired of just standing and watching. He grabbed one of the few survivors of the massacre; a man who was now a prisoner but had been found hiding in his home. The man dropped the handles of his handcart of dead as Pierre took hold of him. Into the man's face Pierre demanded, "Where is he you Pig? Where did you kill him?"

He shook off Constance's hold as she tried to get him to let go. He glared at her and then went back to the stuttering man he held, "Where is he? You killed him so where is he?" Pierre accused.

"Long-shanks, come on." Constance took hold of him again, "You can't blame him for Davy's death."

"Where's his body? You can't say he is dead unless there's a body can you so come on." He turned on her.

"He can't tell you anything so let the man go Pierre."

Reluctantly Pierre let the Jew go and the man grabbed his handcart and hurried on by to the gates. The pair of them looked at the passing bodies before turning to look at each other. Pierre's face fell, "He's dead isn't he? What am I going to tell mother?"

"Don't be silly. You can't say that yet since not all the bodies have been removed. There is still a chance he will appear." Constance said, changing her tune only because it was now Pierre thinking David was dead. Someone needed be hopeful. It was as if he had broken down in heart and mind and was now letting the belief David was dead become true. Though she had thought David dead the day before she wasn't so sure now. Pierre's belief had rubbed off on her. She led Pierre away from the gate and back to the ten.

The small black flies rose up in clouds as Pierre and Constance walked by, disturbing their feed. Scavengers from miles around had come and though stepped away briefly always returned to their chosen meal of the day in human corpses. The stench of decay and skin beginning to cook in the heat was overpowering but somehow Pierre managed to ignore it up to the fiftieth body. At his side all he could hear was Constance gulping to keep the bile down while she held her sleeve over her nose and mouth. There were so many dead and faces were turning blank and featureless so he decided to give up. To Constance at his side he said, "Come on, I can't stand this a moment longer. I know we should try to find him but he is probably half gnawed at already by these animals and that wouldn't look good. He will have lost his life here and will be lost forever here."

She looked relieved to be leaving the corpses behind but tried to hide it for Pierre's sake.

Getting back to their tent the floodgates finally opened for him. He still couldn't believe it in his heart but he knew he had to. David was dead and he had to accept that fact as the truth. The subconscious itch he had felt he decided was what remained of David inside him now that David was gone. It was now time to think about returning home and letting his parents know of David's death. They had to, however, wait for the Duke of Normandy to decide to return home since they had come with him.

Constance cautiously held open her arms and Pierre with gulping sobs leant into her and she closed her arms around him. She held him tight as he let the tears fall like rain on her chest.

Seeing him so miserable she began to cry herself with her chest heaving to hold back her own sobs of grief. Hers slowly died down after the first intense minute and through heavy gulps she attempted to comfort her cousin, "He may be gone from us here in this world but he'll be in Heaven now where he rightfully belongs. He was always an angel Pierre." She remarked thinking about the dirty yellow of David's hair and the calm blue of his eyes.

"He was my brother." Pierre muttered.

"He'll remain in our minds whatever he is… was."

Pierre didn't respond to that for a moment before he said, "I'm going to be left feeling guilty forever." She frowned at that comment, "Why?"

"Because we argued and I let it keep us apart. I should have made up with him while there was a chance and he was willing to become friends again then maybe he would still be alive today." He looked into Constance's concerned face. She gave him a tentative smile as she wasn't sure what Pierre was going to do or say. Looking for more comfort he rested the side of his face on Constance's chest. She gave him a kiss on his head while he recovered from his outburst of crying.

Cautiously Pierre kissed the cloth that covered Constance's breasts as a hand ran round her back and pulled her closer. She didn't resist. The worry and sorrow of a missing David drew them closer together and Constance didn't pull away as Pierre gently pushed her to the ground. There were barely any kisses as Pierre moved down her body and undid both his and her hose. Constance lay still as Pierre used her and it wasn't long before he was spent and he lay on top of her with an occasional tear falling. He rolled off her in a daze. He didn't seem to have any idea of what he had just done. He murmured, "perhaps I should go pray to God to bring David back." As Constance discreetly tidied herself up she replied, "that would be wise." He sighed and got up on to his unsteady feet. He felt dizzy and light-headed after his crying. He looked at Constance and slowly what had just happened came to him. His eyes widened, "did I?"   "It does not matter."

"Yes it does." He dropped to his knees and took her hands, "Connie forgive me."

"You were not in your right mind."

"That is no excuse. What if you become pregnant? I will vow that I will marry you if you do become so and if I do not then may God take me." Pierre got to his feet again and left the tent before Constance could say anything. She hugged herself once he had left. She was unsure how she felt, whether she had been violated or not. She decided that for the moment she would let it go as Pierre was obviously grieving for missing David. It wasn't like it had been rough. She had to hope that she didn't become pregnant and was relieved that Pierre had not noticed that she was no virgin. He need never know that it had been David that had taken it.

Chapter 15

David's rage came to an end when he entered a house and found a family huddled in a corner. Within it was an elderly looking man with two women. The elder had a blue dyed cloth wrapped round her face and was huddling against him with a child in her arms. He sheaved his held sword and sighed, "I can't kill anymore. It is not right to kill people who can't defend themselves. You only live here and it wouldn't have been your decision to stop pilgrims entering the city." None of the three adults knew what he had said but since they had seen him put away his sword the elderly man put hands together and bowed his head as he said in Arabic, "Thank you kind sir, thank you." He cautiously got to his feet and approached David. David held out his hand as he said, "Come no further, remain hidden or you will die by some other's hand." He turned away and left the house.

He climbed on to his horse but then felt a stabbing pain in his right leg. By the light of the near by blazing synagogue fire he saw a sabre welding grim looking young man and on the blade was blood. Looking down to his leg he saw where the edge of the sharp sabre had gone through damaged links of his chain mail legging and gone straight through the muscular flesh of his leg and into his bone. The man shouted up to him in his language of Arabic, "You fiend, killing my family. I'll kill you like you did them." At that moment David's horse gave up and dropped to the ground taking its rider with him. David was too astonished to move and only just made it in time to protect his face from another swing from the sabre toting man. He put an arm up in defence and grimaced as the blade entered the flesh of that also. He searched desperately for his sword at his side but was too slow. As his fingers touched the hilt he fainted.

The Muslim kicked him before entering the house only to be shocked to see his family alive and well. He exclaimed, "I thought he had killed you."

"He didn't. What have you done to him? He was a good man for letting us live." The elder man said as he got to his feet revealing himself to be of an equal height to his son though neither were particularly tall. His hair and beard were growing grey and unlike his son's hands his were small and showed no signs of being used for hard labour. "I have hopefully killed him."

"Not if I can help it. Go out there and bring him here. I will make sure he lives for he shouldn't die. There is no reason for him to."

"He has killed others of us." The younger protested.

"That may be so Zimraan but he has not harmed us so he does not deserve to die by your hand. Bring him here now." "There are others about. What I really should do is get you all out of here." They all froze as they heard horse's footsteps outside but as they passed by Zimraan added, "The streets are covered in blood father, Allah will not be pleased." "It is not our fault so it doesn't matter." Zimraan's father said back, "We will stay here all quiet and hope Allah has something more planned for us. He will protect us and so far he has."

"Father." The younger of the two women murmured. Her father looked to her and she went on, "He must be saved father, I just feel it."

He looked into her eyes and saw her mother within their golden brownness. He gave her a small smile; "Wait patiently. Allah will give him the breath to continue until morning." He looked over to his son as the door to their cellar creaked. Zimraan gestured, "Get down in here and I'll cover it with a rug."

"Not unless you get that man." His nineteen-year-old sister said stubbornly.

"All right, all right; anything for an easy life from both of you." Zimraan sighed,

"Get in there and I'll try and get him in here."

"Thank you Zimraan." His sister smiled and then took her niece and carefully went down the ladder into the cellar followed by her sister-by-marriage.

Zimraan headed to the door and peered out into the early morning light. For the time being no Crusaders were on their street so he slipped out and frowned as he saw two Crusaders lying on the street. Only one was beside a horse so he ran across and pulled helmet and armour off to lighten his load. Finally with it off after a lot of tugging he glanced round the street again before dragging David into the house and down into the cellar where his father exclaimed in a hushed voice, "Be more careful you fool. We don't want him injured anymore than he already is."

It was amazing that no further damage had occurred to David as he was dragged down the wooden steps into the cellar although his head had bounced off every step. The cellar was large and clean. The walls were hidden by shelves filled with dry goods as well as herbs and spices for the old man's medicines as he was a doctor by trade. He was laid out flat on the compact earth floor and the elder man wrapped up the Crusader's leg wound with a piece of wood to hold it straight. Using his daughter's headscarf he wrapped up the arm wound and for the time being hoped that would be enough. He wrapped some of it round the Crusader's head as well as where it was bleeding from the steps. Zimraan

remarked, "Once the slaughtering is over we must get out."
"And how do you plan to do that?" His sister enquired,
"They will kill us instantly if we leave via a gate and if they
find out that we have one of their men."
"I'm thinking Hadiya, give me a chance." Zimraan snapped.
      With such disturbance around him David stirred with
a moan making them nervously look towards him. Once his
eyes focused on the brown faces around him in the light of an
oil lamp he struggled upright and with his good leg pushed
himself away in fear. His head crashed against a shelf and a
pot fell off and knocked him unconscious. Brother and sister
looked to their father and Hadiya asked cautiously, "Will
that…?"

Her father bent over David and in the lamplight carefully had
a look into David's eyes. The pupils adjusted themselves to
the light and with a smile he said, "I think he will live
Hadiya."
   "Why are we doing this? He's one of them and has probably
killed people we know." Zimraan said fiercely, "Why should
I even plan to get him out of the city with us?"
Father and brother looked to Hadiya for an explanation. She
gave them a tight smile,

"I can't explain. We just have to look after him; please
believe me."

   "Whatever. You are making it more difficult for me though.
You may not have anyone but I have my wife and daughter to
consider Hadiya." Zimraan pointed out.
"Why don't we just remain down here? I'm sure the city will
return to normal shortly. They can't all be planning to stay
here and with them gone people will return and they'll need
doctors and they can't chase us from the city since this is a
Holy place for us as well." Hadiya commented.

"Do they know that though?" Zimraan remarked back sharply, "I say we leave the city without him. I'm sure they'll start thieving from homes soon enough and then they'll find us unless we get out. If we do then they'll just find him."

"No you are not going to leave him here." Hadiya protested. "Then explain why."

"You'll never get a husband at this rate with your manner. You should be quiet and obedient like Saree here." Her father commented with sadness in his voice. "I can be so and you know that father but this is one of those moments I can not be what you want me to be. I can't explain why this man must stay with us for Allah hasn't told me the reasons either. I am truly sorry that I cannot tell you father. Maybe the meaning to all this will come clear to us in a dream or vision."

"I think I'm going to have to trust you aren't I?" Her father sighed. Hadiya had at times, like her mother before her, been able to foresee the future through the guidance of Allah. It was never big things, just normal ones such as births, the sex of children or when fruit were rotten on the inside but not showing on the outside.

"Yes and thank you for doing so."

"What your mother would say if she was here I do not know."

"She wouldn't let Hadiya's imagination play games with her. She would also have made sure she was decently covered."

"Now is not the time to be making such remarks Zimraan." The doctor said sternly, "We have to remain together in this time of turmoil and trouble and you aren't making it easy." "Hmpfh." Zimraan crossed his arms and scowled in annoyance, "I am only trying my best to do what is right for us."

"Then think up our escape to my brother's place and it must include this man."

Zimraan vanished from the cellar most of the night and his family thought him out scavenging for food. Mansur abu Zimraan tended to David while he waited for his son to return with Hadiya at his side though there was little either of them could do. At one point she did creep up to get some of his pre-made medicinal mixes. As yet there was no sign of fever on their patient but there was still plenty of time for that to come. Saree sat in a corner with the loose ends of her veil wrapped round her daughter who had fallen asleep. The little girl's mother, however, had no plan to sleep. She sat with wide eyes watching her father-by-marriage and sister-bymarriage tending to the stranger and gently rocking herself and her child to remain calm.

Everyone froze as the door opened above them. Zimraan looked down before descending the steps and bringing the door gently down behind him. His father asked, "What is it like out there?"

"They have stopped for now. A lot are dead. Only a few are left and they have been made to move the dead. I spoke with one."

"Have you food?" Mansur asked.

"Are we to leave this place husband?" Saree asked cautiously from her corner.

"Here is some food." Zimraan drew out stale bread and crumbling goat's cheese from a sack he had obviously picked up from somewhere. He glanced at David before crouching down and tearing the bread up to share amongst them. As he did he began to tell them his plan, "What they are making the prisoners do gave me an idea. Using a handcart I'll pile you up on it like you are dead and take you through the gates and out of Jerusalem. We'll slip away and then we'll be free."

"What about the soldier?" Hadiya asked.

Zimraan sighed, "He'll have to go at the bottom so none of them can see him. If they do see him then we'll be in deep trouble especially if they realise that you are all alive."

"I'm not coming then. I'm not risking the safety of our child Zimraan." Saree said, speaking up for once.

"You are coming Saree and there is nothing you can say or do that will make me change my mind. The more we have the more it will look like you are dead."

Saree hung her head meekly and murmured, "As you wish husband."

"When will we go then?" Hadiya asked, "We should go soon before they find us."

"Let me remind you that I am the head of this family and with such a matter I should be making the decision." Mansur interrupted his two children, "How soon can you get a handcart Zimraan? What are they doing with the dead?"

"I'm sure I'll be able to find one."

"Get out there and find one then. This man…" Mansur gestured to David, "… needs to be moved while he can be."

"I still can't understand why he…?"

"Zimraan." His father said fiercely with warning.

Zimraan scowled, ate the last of his bread and then headed back up and out.

He returned an hour later with a smile on his face. The smiled was all that was needed for them to know he had been successful. He dragged David up the stairs with his father at the bottom saying, "Be careful Zimraan." With David at the top he bent down and took his daughter from Saree's hands and then she and the other two climbed up the steps. They all stood close together while Zimraan looked outside to make sure the coast was clear before returning and dragging David on to the cart. He was more careful with his daughter. Sister and father climbed on willingly. Saree hung back, "Are you sure we'll get through?"

"Yes Saree, now get on." Zimraan ordered his wife sharply, "We don't have all day so hurry up."

Reluctantly she got on and lay still on her side between Hadiya and the side of the cart feeling squashed but not complaining. Her daughter lay between her aunt and grandfather and underneath the light Hadiya was their stranger. Zimraan threw a sack over them the best he could before taking the handles of the cart.

Zimraan pulled them through the streets of Jerusalem trying not to shake them up too much especially as his daughter might cry out in fear and ruin it all. So far she had been quiet as if she understood everything about the situation but since it was his first child he couldn't be sure what she might do. He drew in a deep breath of relief once he had passed under the Gate of the Column. He hissed, "Don't move yet."

His eyes widened at the sight of the rows of dead where the local feral dogs had already appeared with a few jackals not far behind. The vultures, that had always been around, jumped from one clawed foot to another as they hustled back and forth from the corpses with the dogs trying to keep the growing number at bay. The air stank of decaying flesh and on the cart the little girl whimpered at its smell under the sacking. Her grandfather took her small hand and squeezed it, "Sssh little one." He began to murmur a prayer under his breath asking Allah for His protection of them while running his bracelet of beads through his fingers. Once past the corpses, and keeping away from the Crusaders' camp, Zimraan sped up a little so they could reach some type of cover.

Once over the brow of a small hill he stopped. While everyone got off he glanced over the hilltop to make sure they weren't be followed. Turning, he grinned at them, "We've done it."

"Not until we have reached my brother's and that is a day's walk as you know."

Mansur said, "Also they may not have realised yet but when you don't appear back." "They weren't really looking father. They were looking towards their own dead, not us. We are not important to them."

"If that is what you think. Let us get walking then." Mansur said stiffly, "Basimah should ride on the cart."
At hearing that the little girl with her black hair and green eyes clung to her mother even harder and wailed, "Mother, mother."

"She won't be riding on it, not with that man." Saree said sternly.

"He has done neither of you any harm. He could easily have killed you both, all of us, but he didn't, did he?" Hadiya pointed out defensively for David while he couldn't defend himself.

"I am carrying my daughter." Saree said stubbornly.

"You do that then." Hadiya replied. She had never really liked Saree and at that moment she disliked her even more. She went to her father's side as her brother took up the handcart again.

Hussein abu Jalen was up to watch the first stars appear. Compared to his younger brother he was a taller broader shouldered man who had spent his whole life so far in the family home in the family's traditional occupation as a potter. His hair was a lot greyer then Mansur's but though he was older his dark brown eyes were as bright and alert and observant as his brother's. In fact he was a very good potter with a good eye for detail and it showed by the sales to the wealthier houses in the area. His younger brother, in comparison, had been the cleverer of the two which is why he had been sent away to train as a doctor. He was surprised to see a handcart being pulled along with his brother and his family walking alongside it. He called into the house, "Mother, father, Mansur is here."

The men's elderly parents hurried out as fast as they could on arthritic feet feeling both disbelief and joy at seeing their younger son coming towards them. Though the village was only a day's journey away from Jerusalem Mansur didn't visit very often as he was a popular doctor within the city having been trained by one of the best there. Hussein hugged his brother as the group reached him, "I am glad to see you. We feared you might have died in the massacre of our people. Stories are already reaching us of others who have died in the killings. Why has Allah let this happen?" "We were saved uncle." Hadiya said.

"Where is your veil? Have you no idea of modesty and decency?" Her grandmother frowned at her.

"Don't worry about that now Anan." Her husband said, "They will all be tired and will want something to eat and drink I'm sure."

"Here Mansur, who is this?" Hussein asked as he looked into the cart.

"One of them." Zimraan answered for his father in disgust.

"Who?" Hussein's large bearded face frowned.

"One who did the killing."

"He didn't kill us." Hadiya pointed out, "And he's only here because you hurt him when you didn't have to."

"How was I to know that he hadn't?" Zimraan returned sharply.

"Children, please." Mansur said sternly, "Stop this bickering."

"Are you mad Mansur?" His own father demanded.

"It's not me, it was Hadiya and Allah. They are up to something and only Allah at the moment knows what. We need to get him inside and I need to take a proper look at him."

"This is what comes of having a doctor in the family father." Hussein smiled behind his full-face beard, unlike his brother who's was a pointed one on his chin, "You can't stop him from caring for the people, whoever they are."

There was some reluctance from the eldest generation to let the bristly beard David into the two storey family home built round a small working courtyard. Though they were reluctant they couldn't find a reason not to object so Hussein's eldest son, Jalen, and Zimraan carried the Crusader into a small room where Anan hurriedly made up a bed on the straw mattress. She was glad to have her younger son alive but wished there had been more time for her to prepare for their arrival. Already she had got Hussein's wife putting together snacks and making up the tea. She could only hope that Allah had not made Mansur mad for she felt he had more sense then to care for the enemy whether it was Shari'ah or not. Why he had to shown kindness for a man who was obviously an enemy of Islam. There again Allah worked in strange ways.

After having had something to eat and drink Mansur returned to his unconscious patient. Hadiya followed him up shortly once her grandmother had found her a veil to make her decent again. She reluctantly put it on to please her strict grandmother but as she settled down in the small room where the Crusader lay she tucked the veil under her chin instead of having it covering half her face like her grandmother's and Saree's did. She watched her father's back bending over the Crusader and asked, "Will he live?"

"If we look after him well and Allah wishes him to live I think he will." He lifted

David's head gently and put the cup of water he held to the man's partly open mouth.

Most dribbled down from the corner of his mouth and round on to his neck but a little slipped down his throat. Lying the head on the cushion Mansur added, "He has no fever yet but one may come since the sabre that has wounded him was probably dirty. If he lives through the fever then he will live. Fetch me more water Hadi and I'll clean the wounds. The one on his leg worries me the most. The one on his arm looks like it went through an old healed one."

Hadiya got up to do as her father wanted. He watched her go with a tight smile within the neat pointed beard on his chin. She was a pretty woman and though a marriage had been arranged that she had agreed with it had fallen through three years back and no one else had yet to be found as it was put down to her being bad luck that the arrangement had failed. The mid-calf length dress she wore at the moment, made of a light yellow dyed wool suited her. The wide trousers, shalvar, she wore beneath the dress were of the same material and the curve tipped shoes she wore covered her foot up to her ankle, meeting the hem of the shalvar. He wore similar trousers with a tunic over the top and occasionally he wore a long sleeveless coat over that if he was to attend a rich client.

Having cleaned the wounds Mansur left Hadiya to quietly watch over David knowing she could sit up all night with ease while he slept for she had helped him many times with ill patients, especially the women. As he left he said quietly, "If there is any change come and fetch me."   "I know father." She gave him a small smile of the confidence she had in him. Her smile revealed her cheekbones hidden beneath the skin of her face and the dimples she had in her round face. There was nothing overly special about any of her but for the fact her face made her pretty when she smiled and that was quite often. She was a good-natured soul and there was rarely anything that got her down.

Hadiya made sure her father was completely gone before moving closer to the unconscious David to finally get a proper look at him without others watching her moves. Cautiously she opened an eye to see what colour it was and was surprised by the darkness of the blue. Never in her life had she seen anyone with yellow hair and the deep blue eyes he had. There had been pilgrims up to five years back but she had never seen them since her mother had kept her safely hidden away unless shopping and then she had to keep her eyes cast down.

Slowly Hadiya drew a finger down David's brown face and over the obvious cheekbones. Finally she sat back on her heels and sighed. For a moment she wanted to marry him but then she tried to persuade herself that she wouldn't be able to because of their different beliefs and that he probably had a wife somewhere waiting for him to return home. Whatever she was trying to persuade herself about was failing though for she felt Allah wanted the man that lay before her and she to marry.

Living in a Muslim household with little grasp of the language though he was learning David had to settle for their ways of life and that was easy to do since he could not yet go anywhere. He had recovered from his arm injury though the deep one on his leg continued to play up but he was well enough and strong enough.

In the family's opinion he was well enough now to join them in fasting through the day and eating one meal with the descend of the night and another just before the sun rose during the whole of Ramadan. Hadiya attempted to explain the reasoning behind it but with the limited grasp he couldn't understand. The easiest thing was to follow their lead and therefore not offend the family. In some ways it reminded him of lent but better as he could still eat, once it was dark.

On the last night of Ramadan Hadiya boldly took David's hand in front of her father and led him outside, limping. The rest of the family followed behind on to the main and only road of the village. There were greetings from other families who were already out. To David it was all a bit bewildering, as he didn't know why they had all gathered together. Hadiya pointed to the distant horizon and he watched the full moon of a new month rise and was amazed at the brightness of it in the clear sky. At home in England he knew that it was rare to see the moon with all the clouds that liked to hang threatening and morbid in the dull sky. Hadiya smiled at him and he smiled back as he commented, "Beautiful."

"I am glad you think so." She replied, understanding what he had said since he had said it in Arabic, "Tomorrow we go to the Mosque and you must come."

He had understood some and returned, "I can not."

"Why not?"

"Because…" Arabic words failed him though he knew what he wanted to say and that frustrated him and she could see it did.

"I understand I think. It's because you aren't one of us, a follower of Muhammad."

"Yes." He smiled with relief, "I don't know the ways either."   "Father can show you." She said encouragingly.

"I don't think it would be right." He turned his head away from her.

She sighed, "I understand."

"Thank you." He turned back to look at her face and gave her a tight smile.

He waited at the family home for them to return from the Mosque. He could hear them before he saw them and it reminded him of the fact he was in a distant land far away from his family and true home. Small presents were given out and he was surprised to receive two himself and wished he had something to give back had he known that gift giving was what happened to celebrate the end of Ramadan. He thanked Hadiya and her father for the two gifts and tried to explain that he would have given something in return had he known. He hoped they got the gist of it for they seemed to with their nods of apparent understanding. He gave them a tight smile and wished he was anywhere but in the confusing world of a Muslim family.

During a quiet moment Hadiya said to her father, "Can I speak with you?" "On what daughter?" He asked though his eyes were on David as the man attempted to have a conversation with Hussein.

"About Da'ud father."

He turned and looked at her, "Da'ud? Why?"

"You know I couldn't explain why he was important I now understand." "You do?" He looked surprised. She nodded, "Allah, I feel, has given me the reasons." "And what is that?" Mansur enquired fearfully.

"Father..." She paused a minute to find the courage to go on, "Father... I want to marry him, marry Da'ud." Close by Zimraan had heard all of it and joined in the conversation, "You aren't going to marry him Hadiya. I won't agree anyway. He killed our people father and he isn't one of us. You can't let her father." He protested to Mansur who remained calm. Silent hung over them for a short while as Mansur thought it all through. He knew he'd rather have his daughter marry someone she liked and was close to her age then someone she would never get along with like the simpleton of four months back. Hadiya grew more and more nervous as the silence continued and she realised she had been holding her breath as she gulped for air at her father's voice, "No Zimraan. Hadiya, I will agree to such a marriage if he wishes to marry you. Also he must become one of us. If both of those are met and I have a feeling that they will, then you may become his wife."

Hadiya beamed at her father, "Thank you." She gave his cheek a loving kiss and then headed back to Da'ud to speak with him.

"Are you mad?" Zimraan exclaimed at his father, "Some demon has addled your mind."

"Let me just say son that I feel Allah put those words on my lips."

"Then you don't want it to happen?"

"I did not say that."

"She won't manage it." Zimraan sneered.

"Come, you know your sister better then that. She will do it I feel because Da'ud will let her. He is drawn to her like any single man, or married at that, is. I think he will be able to control her with his calm influence."

"I think you talk nonsense father."

"Do not speak to me like that." Mansur said sternly, "Respect your parents as I and your mother taught you to and respect my opinion. You may have your own but here mine rules, do you understand?" he held a finger pointed at his adult son.

"Yes." Zimraan said with worry that his father may disown him.

"Good, then let her try without you trying to thwart her attempts. This is Allah's doing and we can not interfere in this."

"I'm not going to accept him as family." Zimraan said stubbornly.

"I'm not expecting you to do that just yet but if it works I will expect you to accept him as a member of this family."
"We will see."

"Go, before you make me any angrier." Mansur said fiercely and Zimraan sulkily left.

An animated conversation was going on between Hadiya and David though

she was doing most of the talking while he tried to keep up with the translating in his mind. Half the time he was nodding in pretence that he understood. Finally she stopped, "Well?"
"Err... well..." He frowned as he tried to think of something.

"Would you like us to be husband and wife?"

"I don't know... I know barely any of your ways Hadiya."

"The imam can teach you and I can."
"I know little of your tongue."
"You can do it Da'ud. You have done well so far." She said encouragingly and smiled hopefully, "Well?"
"I won't agree to marriage, is
that how you say it?" She nodded.
"I will learn your ways and the teachings of your Muhammad and then..."

"Then?" She looked hopeful. "And then we will see."

She felt slightly downcast at that but knew she was going to have to accept that for the time being.

"I'm sorry I can't agree to anymore." He looked sorrowful himself and reached out to touch her. She shuffled along a little and then got to her feet from the bench, "I understand that one step at a time is better then all at once between us."

Chapter 16

David had been preparing for this one moment for the last three weeks with Hussein helping him. Already he had decided that before marrying Hadiya he had to make it worth her while and make sure she had a comfortable life.

Hussein was throwing some pottery for David to sell on and make some money to go on to the next stage of his plan. His plan seemed to have been leaked out however and he found the whole of the small village community knowing. At the village's new year celebrations he was given two rarely used camels by one man, the carpenter offered to make shelves and furniture once he had himself a house and/or shop. Farmers were willing to trade with him, sell their goods on to him and others just gave David advice. He felt overwhelmed by it all for never had he met men so eager to help without wanting something in return. He promised them that if they ever needed help then he would do so. They just nodded and smiled at that, not saying anything to give away whether they had accepted it or not. To them they liked the fact David was willing to try and make a life for himself and to see if Allah dained him fit enough to marry Hadiya. It was a test in their view and they wanted to help him past it since they could see Hadiya wanted to be with him and he was showing a growing interest in her in return.

Before Hadiya found out by someone who was not him David decided he should talk with her so he took her to a quiet corner of the courtyard though still in full view of everyone else so no suspicions were created. Everyone hung back as if they understood David's need for privacy with

Hadiya for the moment. She looked into his face with a look of adoration in her eyes and a small smile playing on her lips. He took her hand cautiously as he said in slightly stilted Arabic, since over the last six months it had greatly improved; "I must go away but I will return in a year. I need to make a name for myself and get some money. I don't have my share of the riches anymore. I want to create a life that you would wish to live in for no one wants to be poor."

"I would live with nothing to our names as long as I was with you."

"Your father would say differently I feel. I will do all I can because I want to be with you for life but if I return unsuccessful then Allah obviously doesn't want us to be together. Do you understand Hadiya?" He gave her an intense look of hope and concern.

"I understand Da'ud." She smiled sweetly at him, "But I'm sure Allah will make you successful."

"God willing Hadiya, God willing." He gave her a tight smile.

"I have confidence in you and I'm sure Allah does as well otherwise he wouldn't have let you live. Your namesake did well for himself especially as he was the one to build Jerusalem as you saw it and he wasn't even royal to begin with. He overcame a large problem and you will too, I'm sure. What do you plan to do so I can listen out for your name?"

His smile became easier and he murmured, "Goliath".

She frowned at him but he just continued to smile before answering her question, "This and that; I'm not really sure at the moment since I need to get some money together. Somehow I will sell things to the Crusaders who have remained here."   "The enemy?"

"Hadiya, you must understand something." He sighed. "What?" she looked enquiringly into his face. He turned away and looked at his feet and wiggled his toes. She reached out with a hand and turned his face so he once again looked at her. She gave him an encouraging smile as she asked, "What must I understand?"

"You could say I am the enemy."

"No you aren't." she protested.

"Hadiya, I have killed many of your..., our people; the followers of Mohammad. I am a Crusader, the enemy, the invaders. We came to claim what we thought Jesus Christ and ours's; Jerusalem. We didn't know it to be a holy city for you as well though I know that now."

"You talk as if you are one of them still." She said feeling slightly hurt, "What are you?"

"It takes more than a few months to erase the memories of twenty-five years as a Christian Hadiya. I may have turned completely Muslim to all appearances but inside there are still some of the beliefs of a Christian. They were my people for the whole of the campaign and somewhere out there I have a brother and cousin who probably think me dead."   "You said they were your people. Who are your people now?" she asked out of curiosity.

He looked into her face that revealed nothing but a pair of brown blinking eyes. He sighed, "I'm not one of them any more but I'm not one of you either. I sit in the middle. I'm a misfit for the time being waiting to see which way I go next. All I can say is that I can approach the Crusaders because I can speak their language and know their ways and there will always be something they want. I will sell them pottery, furniture, brass, cloth, food, salt, spices and wine. I plan to have contacts everywhere including back in the countries I have left behind."

Her eyes had grown wide at this while he went on, "I begin at the bottom with the help of your uncle but I will rise and people will know my name and Renard will be known and once again I will have brought honour to my name. I won't let greed take control of me though. For all those who help me I will repay them and I will help the poor as Mohammad says we should and because it's the right thing to do. Treat those around you how you would like to be treated the Bible says. One day those you have helped might be the ones helping you if you were to fall on hard times."

"Da'ud you are so considerate." She smiled warmly at him, loving him even more since he seemed so knowledgeable on life and how he made the life appear so much better then it was in reality. She clutched his arm. "You will be successful, I just feel it and I'm glad Allah let you live through my father's skill as a doctor."

"You know, I don't think I ever truly thanked him. I'll go now."

"A year Da'ud. That is a long time." She pointed out wistfully.

"I'm sure you can wait and really if you are busy it flies by. I will come and see you next New Year's day, God willing. Now, I must go to your father and speak with him." He got to his feet and she looked up to him and said, "Good luck Da'ud."

"Thank you."

It seemed both men were on the search for the other and both smiled at the sight of the other. Both tried to speak but ended up laughing. David said with respect, "You go first sir."

"Come with me then." Mansur beckoned David to follow him. David felt a little confused but did as he was told. In Mansur's bedroom the man took up a small cloth parcel. He turned back to David, "let me give you a little something Da'ud before you go."

"There is no need to sir. You have already done enough for me. That is what I wanted to talk about. I wanted to thank you for having made me well again."

"It was Allah's will that you lived through my hands."

"One day I hope to be able to repay you for with the wounds I had I could easily have died."

"How are they? I know the leg one was the worse I have ever seen. I should really apologise for what my son did."
"You should not need to sir. I can forgive him easily for I think I would have done the same if I had believed my family killed by the man who had just stepped out of my home." Mansur gave the younger man a warm smile, "You may reject it but you must accept this gift." He pressed the gift into David's hands. David cautiously opened the fabric up and looked at the ninety-nine bead stringed together and knew exactly what they represented. Each of the beads on the Tasbih represented a name of God, Allah.   "I couldn't."

"You must and take this money as well otherwise you will never be able to do anything."   "I…"

"Father, why are you doing this?" Zimraan exclaimed from the door.

"How long have you been there?" Mansur demanded, fuming, "Can I not have a private talk with another person? You should respect me like Da'ud here does."
"He's not one of us father."

"He is one of us, he has learnt our ways and Mohammad's teachings."

"He wants to trick us and send us to our deaths."

"I don't wish to do that Zimraan." David said calmly, not letting Zimraan get to him.
"Don't call me that, you have no right to." Zimraan said fiercely to David.

"I can give gifts to who I want Zimraan." Mansur said sternly and with a warning in his voice, "I believe he is a good man and Allah does as well otherwise he would not have become well in my care."

"Hmpfh." Zimraan replied and had no plan to go anywhere just yet making David feel like a conman though he wasn't. Mansur didn't tell either of the men to go as he moved round the room in search of other things. Mansur unbent himself with a smile and turned away from the simply made chest against the wall of his bedroom, "Da'ud, I also wish to give you this."

In his hand he had a large piece of cloth and he added, "Bend you head so I can put this on."

David obeyed and Mansur put the folded triangular cloth on David's head and then wrapped the thin leather strap called the 'iqal round to hold the cloth in place.

"Sir…." David said, "You can't do this."

"It's God wish that I do all this and only he knows why I do so. This…" He gestured to what David was now wearing, "This will help you, protect you from the burning sun. With those two camels I'm sure there will be some travelling. It can keep you cool during the day and warm at night. You can cover your face if a dust storm comes your way. There will be travelling I feel at the beginning to get what you want." He gave David a warm fatherly smile, "And if Allah wills it we will be seeing you again soon."

"A year."

"A year it is then. You are going to leave now?"

"Where will I find you in a year?" David enquired just to be on the safe side.

"If it is New Year's Day then we are all likely to be here but if not I plan to be in

Jerusalem. I am going to return there with Hadiya and…"
"I'm not returning with you father." Zimraan announced.

Mansur turned to his son with a frown, "What is this Zimraan?"

"It will be filled with the enemy and it won't be safe. My family is important to me and I'm not having them killed father."
"If that is what you wish son but you know where you'll find me; in the same home as ever which hopefully no one has taken."
"I will find you somehow." David remarked with a smile.

"We'd best let you leave now." Mansur remarked.

        Murmurs rose as David re-appeared in the courtyard. They all approved of his appearance. With his headdress along with the clothes he wore he looked like he had always lived within a day's walk from Jerusalem. Men shook his hands and hugged him as he passed through the courtyard. There were smiles all round though the women hung back watching quietly. The children ran out ahead of David and the men to where the two camels lay on their knees and tethered. Their jaws moved from side to side as they chewed. Hussein smiled, "We will hear about how successful you are I'm sure."

"God willing." David smiled back.

"I'll make you as much pottery as you need."

"You can't do that Hussein or you'll lose money."

"A friend in need is important. Good luck." He hugged David, "Keep yourself well." Zimraan appeared and David held out his hand but the other turned his nose up at it. David saw he would never get along with Zimraan and decided he wasn't going to let it bother him. There were too many other things to worry about then one man's disliking of him. He shrugged his shoulders at Zimraan to show he didn't care.

He pulled the camels to their feet by their rope halters. As an afterthought before he left completely he turned and said, "Thank you for everything you have done. If I don't return do not think I didn't appreciate it all. I have never known any people so willing to welcome a stranger into your lives though he was not of you; thank you. If I am successful I will repay you for all you have done for me." He smiled at them all and then turned round and tugged at his two reluctant camels.

Hadiya waited quietly and when she saw everyone return to her grandparent's courtyard she slipped out. She ran after David's slow moving figure and when she reached him touched him. He jumped and turned to her and saw her gasping laughing face with her veil lying limply down her back and her long plait of black hair over a shoulder. He remarked, "You really surprised me."

"How could I have? I know I was making a lot of noise."

"I just fell into deep thought for what lies ahead of me." He explained, "What are you doing here anyway? Shouldn't you be back celebrating and being a good Muslim woman?"   "I don't mean to offend but I don't care about being a perfect Muslim woman. I want to be able to be myself sometimes."

"And this is one of those moments?" He enquired with a smile.

"Yes." She admitted easily but shied away from looking him in the eyes. She was being daring in her actions and feared what she was about to do would go the wrong way. He waited patiently for her to say something and was surprised when she reached up and put her lips on his. His arms went round her and he pulled her closer.

Reluctantly she pushed herself away from him and both pairs of eyes were bright. He asked, "What was that for?"

"That was my first time and I don't want to kiss anyone else but you Da'ud."

"Is that a good thing?" He teased.

She frowned and then smiled, "Yes. Do come back. I won't care if you aren't successful."

"If I'm to get more of those sudden kisses I will be back." He smiled, "You should go back and I should get going." He bent and kissed her cheek. She put her hand to the cheek as she watched him continue on his way.

Chapter 17

April 1101

Hadiya was dressed in gold and red for her wedding day as she stood before David. The dowry David was to pay to Hadiya had been argued out between David and Mansur and an agreed amount decided upon which would be Hadiya's. For the time being they were all at the potter's house with the courtyard decorated with flowers and everyone was dressed in their best. Before the ceremony David remarked to Hadiya making her blush and bow her head to hide it in her cheeks, "You are looking sensational." "Thank you." She murmured.

Everyone had accepted the marriage that was about to happen including Hadiya of course. For reasons of his own Mansur felt that it should be done in the presence of a mosque representative, an imam, since David hadn't always been a Muslim; though he didn't have to be there. David understood and didn't object as the elected man appeared at his and Hadiya's side. They both looked at the man as each of them were asked three times for their consent to the wedding. The rings were then exchanged with Hadiya smiling with pleasure as David puts hers on her ring finger.
They bowed their heads as the imam placed hands on them and blessed them.

Hadiya clung to David's arm as he signed the contract with Mansur. Hussein and the village carpenter acted as witnesses over the signing as he was a good family friend. With it done he shook hands with his father-in-law and then smiled at Hadiya.

She commented, "I am happy to be yours Da'ud."

"And I am glad you are my wife." He kissed her softly on the lips.

"What will happen now Da'ud? Jerusalem is a day away."

"Then a day away it is. We begin the journey now Hadi and when we reach your new home we will feast and everyone will be welcome because I won't mind celebrating my marriage with them all. You have made me feel happy and complete." He smiled warmly at her.

For a brief moment he thought of his brother. He wondered then how his brother was doing, if he had married or not back home. He knew Pierre had got home though he couldn't explain how. He considered at the time that perhaps he should send a message but then decided not to. He felt sure that his family would disapprove of his new life and religion. If he did return home there would only be the monastery or being a paid soldier in someone's retinue.

"Thank you and will I get to meet Qudamah?"

"He disappeared off north to trade but hopefully he should be back. Don't you worry, you'll meet him in time." He put an arm round her and drew her close to him.

Everyone from the village was behind them while David led them with Hadiya riding his mare. She felt like the only woman in the world as she rode through Jerusalem with people moving out of the way to make way for them. David frowned as he heard a shout, "Come back here you scoundrel!"
A boy swept pass with a man close behind. Qudamah skidded to a halt in front of David and his face changed from one of anger to a beaming smile, "Da'ud. Don't leave me in charge again."
"I didn't Qudamah. I thought you were away north."

"I was but now I'm not. I wanted to meet your blushing bride before she loses all ability to blush. Is this her?" Qudamah asked as he looked to Hadiya on the horse who was blushing. Hadiya returned, "You must be Qudamah?"

"That I am." He smiled with the laughter lines around his dark brown eyes deepening. His face was browner than anyone else's she had ever seen as he had the black blood of Africa in him and spent more days in the sun then out of it. He was a large bulky man but though he was strong he had never hurt a fly. His black hair was greying in places but he hadn't let age knock him down. Qudamah asked, "You are the woman he waited a year to marry? Personally I would have married you instantly."

"You keep your eyes on your animals Qudamah." David warned, "Anyway, where is Mohammad?"

"His wife was giving birth Da'ud. That's what he claimed anyway."

"That is very possible Qudamah. I'm sure he'll re-appear." David replied as Qudamah walked the last few feet to his home.

Mohammad was there, a wiry looking man but a cheerful one and healthy as well. He was stronger then he looked and intelligent. Unlike David and Qudamah he could write which was the main reason he had been hired. He was also a devoted family man with two daughters and another child just born. He appreciated working for David and Qudamah who were both good men in turn. All three of them got on well. David enquired, "Where were you? You know Qudamah can't handle the customers."

"Hey?" Qudamah objected.

"I am sorry Da'ud sir. My wife was giving birth."

"I should congratulate you then I suppose. Boy or girl?"
"Boy sir and is this your wife?" Mohammad looked to
Hadiya.

"There are two reasons to celebrate then is there not?"
David smiled, "Let a sheep be killed for the poor.
Mohammad can I trust you to buy one?"
"Of course you can." Mohammad smiled. David found his
purse of money and handed it over to the man and remarked,
"You and your wife must come to dinner." "I'm sure she
would be delighted to, thank you sir." He grinned at his
employer and then headed away to do as David wanted.
        With Mohammad gone David helped Hadiya down
from his horse and Qudamah took the reins as he said, "I'll
see you in a few minutes, don't do anything too exciting until
I'm back."
"Of course not." David replied and watched the man go.
Qudamah had become a close friend that was the closest to
replacing Pierre as a brother. Hadiya could sense the
closeness between them as David led her through the shop
that had pots, rolls of fabric and hemp sacks of spices and
large carpets hanging from the walls. There was also a piece
of furniture that need to be delivered by Mohammad. At the
back were two barrels of wine in the deep dark recesses of the
shop to remain cool next to some salt. He led her through into
the back where the house seemed to grow larger as a second
floor was revealed and she remarked, "He appears like a
brother to you. What about your real one?"
"Pierre will always be my true brother and Qudamah is a
close friend and will never replace him." David replied
though for a moment he wondered how honest that was.
Pierre was one person, his blood kin, but had Qudamah and
Hadiya together actually replaced him considering how far
away his brother was? "now, welcome to your new home;
well for a short while anyway. Shortly, hopefully, we will

move to a large place where Qudamah will have a room or two with us. Mohammad will come and live here to make life easier for him especially as he lives in a two room rented home at the moment and that's probably beginning to feel crowded."

"You appear to be a good employer."

"I hope I am." David smiled, "And I hope I'll be a good husband as well." "I know you'll be a good one for you are an all round good man Da'ud." She smiled warmly at him. "I hope we'll be happy together Hadi."

"I am sure we'll be so."

She let him place his cracked lips on hers. She closed her eyes and allowed the sensations from such a gentle loving kiss run through her.

Since it was heading into the early evening he organised where everyone was sleeping with help from Mansur and Qudamah and their homes. No one wanted to really leave but they knew with the new day they would return for the feast that was almost ready. The women had prepared most of it and all that needed to be done was cook the food and once started that wouldn't take long. With farewells until the morning David led Hadiya to his bedroom. From shyness they turned their backs on each other as they undressed. Hadiya slipped under the blanket first and from embarrassment at never seeing a man naked at all in her life, not even her brother, she closed her eyes as David turned and got into bed himself. He turned on to his side and lay with head resting in his hand, braced by his elbow. He smiled at her softly while she held the blanket up to her neck. He reached over with his free hand and gently took the blanket. She clutched at it for a moment and then let it go. She held herself stiffly and asked cautiously, "Do you know what to do?"

"I'll go gently." He gave her a tight smile. Lazily he began to draw rings round her closest breast with a finger as he commented, "I began to love you from the moment I first heard your name. I didn't know that truly then but now I do." His smile softened and she returned it. He paused and studied her. She looked at his calm face and asked, "What should we do then? My mother never told me, and my grandmother just didn't think about it. She is growing forgetful in her old age but that can't..."

"They don't matter. Let us see each other to remove your embarrassment. You are a woman and I am a man and we were born the way we are, everything each of us have is natural and Allah created us that way for our set purposes in life."

"I understand." She whispered from nerves, "If you know what happens will you help me?"

"Of course." He was pleased she had admitted that she wanted help and to understand. He bent and kissed her. He drew the blanket down to look at her completely and so she could look at him. Whereas she had admitted not knowing he knew something for he had visited a few brothels over the past year though he would never tell her.

She looked up at him patiently waiting for him to make the first move. He was cautious with his rough skinned fingertips at first and slowly explored her body by the lamplight in a way he had never done before. She drew in her breath in fear and then relaxed as she could sense tenderness in his touching. Shyly she reached up and touched his face with both hands and then his chest and down to his groin. They were slow and steady together.

He stirred in the early morning and found Hadiya giving him a small smile in the early light and lamplight. He turned on to his front from his side and put an arm over her. She looked at the arm with its two scars and asked, "Where did the other scar come from Da'ud?"

He opened his eyes again for a brief moment and answered sleepily, "Some battle."

"What one?"

"Can't remember." He murmured as his eyes sank shut. She sighed and allowed him to sleep though she held on to his hand and played with his fingers. She was feeling wideawake and couldn't get back to sleep like David seemed to be able to do. She kissed the hand and closed her eyes in the hope of falling asleep again.

It was Qudamah who woke them, cheerfully announcing to the sleeping couple as he entered the room, "You can't sleep all day you two. There is celebrating to do. Come on, up you get lazy bones."
David turned over and slowly sat up, "Qudamah, what are you doing here? Have you been...?"

"Who do you think I am?" Qudamah looked horrified, "Of course not but you have to get up. The guests are waiting for you and your pretty bride here..." Hadiya turned over and a leg appeared from under the blanket making Qudamah smile, "Nice leg."

"Watch it." David warned his friend but smiled as well, "Thank you."

"You coming then?"

"Give me a few minutes to wake my wife here."
"I'll go tell them then." Qudamah beamed and headed from the room.

As they came down the stairs and were spotted Mansur got to his feet and greeted David,
"Ah, here comes my favourite son-in-law."

"I believe I am your only son-in-law." David returned with a smile.

"They are mere details. Come and sit with Hadi in pride of place. Food is being cooked and will soon be here." All the men were already seated. Zimraan sat at the far end looking like he wished to be somewhere else but since father and grandfather had ordered him to attend there was nothing he could do but sulk. Once David was seated Mansur quietly questioned in his ear so his daughter didn't hear, "Nothing wrong with my daughter I hope? She was…?"
David broke into the other's fears and quietly replied, "There was nothing wrong and yes she was. I am pleased with her of course. All we can now do is pray to Allah for a child to be born."

"Of course, good." Mansur said in his normal smile as the smile returned to his face and he gave it to his daughter as well as David, "I am proud of you Hadi."
"Yes father." She
felt a little confused but there again she hadn't heard the words murmured between Mansur and David though she was sat close to them.

Chapter 18

August 1149

     It was pass midnight by the time the party to celebrate Pascal's arrival calmed and the large family made their way to their beds. Pascal could only look on with amazement in his eyes that such a large family could be so close and be able to laugh and tease with such ease and familiarity. There was a warmth that was perhaps missing from his own small one. He actually felt jealous from what he was witnessing. It was only once he lay beside his son and surrounded by youths and boys that he properly began to consider all that had been told especially as he couldn't get to sleep even though the day had been a long one and full of eye-popping surprises. Midway through the evening Pascal made up his mind that David Renard was obviously the man he had been sent to find by his mother. It was with slight trepidation that he handed the letter over to his uncle. David was surprised to be given a letter, "what is this?"

"My mother said I should give it to you and that I wasn't allowed to open it." David turned it over and over in his hands and peered at the seals keeping the letter firmly shut. He glanced up at Pascal, "I guess you want to know what has been written?"

"Well…" Pascal didn't want to admit it but he was extremely curious. David smiled with amusement as he broke the seals open. His smile began to fade as he read the words that Constance had dictated to a scribe. Seeing the smile vanish Pascal asked with concern, "What's wrong?"

"You'd best go."

    "Go?"

"I just need some time on my own." David explained as he folded the letter back up so that as Pascal stood the man couldn't see its contents. Pascal asked, "Is everything all right?"

"Umm… I'll let you know later."

With Pascal gone David opened the letter again. As he read it for a second time he held his breath in the hope that the letters did not spell out what he had already read. It was with a long sigh that he folded the letter and tucked it into the folds of his clothes. For the moment he decided not to mention the contents to Pascal.

First he needed to speak with Hadiya.

With the rest of the family in bed quiet had descended on the Renard household and David finally had time to speak with Hadiya on a subject he really didn't want to bring up as he had never mentioned it before. Thankfully Hadiya broached the subject as David pretended to be asleep. As he closed his eyes she shook him, determined to find out what had gone on between her husband and their guest which had turned him sombre for the rest of the evening, "Da'ud, speak to me. What was so important about this man that you had to have a private conversation? Why is he staying here as well? We barely have enough room with everyone here." "He has a name Hadiya."

"I heard that. Is he your brother's son? Has your brother died?"

David shook his head, "He is sort of Pierre's."

"How can he be sort of? He's either your brother's or he's not."

"I can't really explain."

Hadiya sat up and looked intently at him by the light of a single oil lamp, "I have been married to you for a long time and I know when something is wrong. You weren't completely there during the celebrations. You were unnerved and I could see you glancing at that man."

"Pascal." He put in sharply, "He has a name."

"You were shaken up as if something was wrong. What is wrong? Please tell me." She implored him. He sighed, "He is not Pierre's by blood."

"He isn't?"

"He is…" He hesitated in telling her but decided to get it out to stop her nagging,

"He's mine."

Her mouth opened but nothing came out as she was in shock. She felt betrayed and muddled. How could he have done such a thing?

Hoping he would not have to explain himself to her any further for the time being he turned his back to her. She remained sitting up and staring across the room. Finally she spluttered, "How? Why? Who?"

"It happened before we took Jerusalem with Constance."

"But it was incest." Hadiya pointed out.

"Not really as she is not my real cousin."

"Still, how could you?!"

"It just happened." David replied meekly. There really wasn't any way of explaining the event away.

"I don't want the details." She exclaimed as she got out of bed, "I can't sleep with you tonight."

"Hadiya." He pleaded as he sat up and watched her go.

"Don't change my mind tonight Da'ud." She said firmly and left the room leaving

David feeling hurt and desperate to get her love back

He wished the son by Constance had never appeared so he would never have had to explain it to Hadiya. He got out of bed and headed out to find Hadiya. He saw her sitting on the edge of the fountain with hands to her face. He headed down the stairs and crossed to her. He sat down beside her and cautiously put a hand on her knee, "I'm sorry I never told you. I just didn't want to hurt you. I felt no need to tell you." It was one moment, a long time ago, that he had forgotten about though it clearly had consequences for Constance. He gave her a tight smile though she couldn't see it in the dim courtyard where the beginnings of the new day were slowly appearing. He removed his hand from her knee and looked down at his bare feet, "I didn't even know he existed, or he had even been conceived."

"Sssh, it's all right but I think we need to get back to bed before we embarrass the family." She smiled, not believing herself to be so soft with David and forgiving him far too easily, "Obviously Allah wanted you to do it." She placed a loving kiss on his cheek as she put her arms around him, "Maybe Allah has pardoned you for such a sin, if it was one. Look around you there is proof that it was not a sin. Come, it was obviously nature taking control for that one moment in time. Is she angry with you?" "No." He didn't mention the fact that she had written that she loved him even though she had married Pierre.

"Then don't worry about it. She obviously doesn't regret having your child and is not think it was a sin." "But still, it should never have happened."

"It can not be helped now. Why start worrying about it all over again? Come, I am sorry about earlier, I was just shocked that there was a son created from before we were married." She pulled him to his feet, "We should probably get back to bed." She gave him a soft smile. Once on his feet he pulled her to him and murmured, "What would I do without you?"

"Well, you would have died at my brother's hand." She replied matter-factly, "come on, lets get back to bed there is a chill in the air. Are you going to tell him?"   "I don't know whether I should or not."

"Just do what you think right."

"I will try." David sighed as he climbed the steps behind his wife. His mind briefly wandered back to that moment of uncontrollable lust with Constance but with a shake of his head he sent it back to the depths of his memory where it belonged. It was not a moment in his life that he was proud of even if Constance was not bothered by it.

Chapter 19

September 1149

They visited the birthplace of Jesus Christ and then returned to Jerusalem to the place of most importance for Christians. The Church of the Holy Sepulchre sat upon the tomb of Christ. The church had been rebuilt after the destruction of it in 1009 by Fatimid Caliph al-Hakin and it had only recently been finished in the Norman style. David hung back as they reached the Church. He realised he was being foolish to even attempt to enter though he had once been Christian. Pascal looked to him, "Are you coming in?"

"I don't know now." He didn't go on as he didn't want to reveal to his son that he was a Muslim for fear of the reaction. "Don't you dare enter that church heathen!" A voice shouted and turning David saw three troublemakers, new visitors in the city who had come with the latest crusaders thinking the city needed to be saved. They had come seeking him out to do business as he had been recommended until they found out his religion, "stop trying to convert us. You should get out of the city." David put a hand on his knife.

"Come in with me uncle." Pascal suggested softly especially as he didn't want to see his uncle hurt by the three men. "You are a bigamist." Another of the three shouted, "Two wives and a mistress. Pure

Norman blood and a dirty old man!"

David was shaking from fear for never had he been insulted so badly. With this going on he really didn't know what to do especially as Gallien was looking on in puzzlement.

"Get away from here and stop polluting our church and city. You don't belong here. We've warned you enough and this time you aren't going to get away easily and then we will kill your family so you can all go to Hell together." The third put in and at Pascal said, "Don't protect him, he doesn't deserve it. Get away from him before he takes you to Hell with him."

"Leave him be." Pascal said with warning.

"Chums are we?" The first sneered.

"Leave it be." David murmured to his son and put a hand on him.

The three men drew closer and Gallien actually stepped backwards feeling he didn't really want to be involved even though he should do so to even up the two sides. He had no weapon anyway. David drew out his knife to defend himself and wished he was younger. Seeing his uncle do so Pascal drew out his own knife and looked at Gallien sternly to tell him to do the same. Gallien reluctantly drew his out as the three men brought out some of their own.

If it wasn't for two monks who had come out from the church to find out what the shouting was about a fight would have broken out. The three troublemakers scowled and put their knives away before running off. The two monks approached the three Renards with one enquiring, "Were they bothering you?"

"Thank you for coming out when you did." Pascal said with relief and a smile. "They are always causing trouble especially for the Renard family which is a shame for they do no one any harm."

"That doesn't mean anything." The other remarked sharply, "Those Renards are still heathens and shouldn't even be inside the city walls. They pollute the city and endanger it. With them in here demons are welcome."

"Ignore him. Come, do come in." The first said brightly.

"Err…" Pascal glanced at his uncle and then went on, "Another time but thank you."

"Everyone is welcome. Mass is held here."

"I'll remember that." Pascal answered with a tight smile. What he wanted to do was get his uncle home and find out why he was getting attacked and what the second monk had meant by his comments.

He got David home and helped him down into his seat since it looked like the old man had shaking legs that wouldn't hold him up. David took the incident with good humour, "That was a bit too close for comfort."

"That was far too frightening. You should stay here."

"It's just words Pascal. I've never been up to the church before. I'm not going to let them get to me and neither should you."

"Are they always that bad?"

"I told you it doesn't matter."

"Why were they saying such things?" Gallien asked with wide eyes.

Pascal looked at Gallien and then at David. His son had managed to ask the question that he had wanted to. David looked uncomfortable and looked at his feet, "There is something I have not told you and I am surprised you have not noticed either."

"Noticed what?" Gallien demanded, "They were threatening you."

"I am one of the enemy, I'm a Muslim."

"One of those Mohammed worshippers?"

"No. We worship Allah, God. We do not worship our prophet."

"It makes no difference you are still one of them." Pascal said with shock. It felt like half of his world had suddenly crashed around him. It couldn't be right. Had he made a huge mistake and this man wasn't his uncle, "this can't be right?" "I am not lying." David answered calmly.

"That explains that then." Gallien remarked

Looking at his son Pascal couldn't believe how calm he was taking it, definitely different from him. He enquired, "You have nothing to say about it?"

"You were the one who wanted to come, not me. If he was a Muslim worthy to be an enemy of then I would be shocked and angry but really I've had no impression that they are bad. The Moors surrendered graciously so they can't all be barbarians and they worship God so..." Gallien shrugged his shoulders, "Like he said the Jews are our enemy, they sent Jesus to his death. Jews are the ones they should be banishing from the city."

"As a Muslim Jesus is actually known as a prophet but Mohammad is our main one like Jesus is for you." David pointed out before an argument arose between father and son and encouraged by Gallien response.

"There's nought wrong really then is there." Gallien commented back and looked at his father. His eyes wandered as he saw a young woman, a year younger then himself, appear from the kitchen. She smiled shyly at him and he did the same back but then turned back to the two men as David remarked, "Don't let me put you off going back to the church, you should go."

"I don't know."

"Once home we may never get another chance father." Gallien pointed out. "Well... I suppose... You don't mind?" Pascal asked of his uncle though he was still shocked by David's religious admission.

"I would just be in the way. Go and get some spiritual blessing." David smiled encouragingly.

Pascal and Gallien entered the rotunda where ancient Roman temple pillars had been halved to hold up the gold and white dome, which reflected the soft oil lamp light back down so that the monks and pilgrims could guide themselves to the caves, the Holy Sepulchre, where Jesus was buried before he rose again. The two Renards solemnly touched the rough-hewn walls of the burial chamber. Leaving it they went to the Calvary, an altar placed over the site of the crucifixion cross. Both men knelt before the altar to pray. Pascal was more intent on praying then his son who was quietly looking around and taking in the mosaic of Jesus above the altar in a gold mosaic frame.

Throughout the church complex there were mosaics and imagery that was bright from it all being so new. As well there were pillar capitals retelling tales from the Old Testament. Around the two men as well as other pilgrims there was the soft songs of the monks and clergy that were there to maintain the buildings and shrines as well as to religiously help the pilgrims in confessions and blessings. Through all of it they were silent as if the place was to sacred for words to be spoken which would disturb the Holy air dusted with incense. To Pascal it felt like he was the closest to Heaven he would ever get until he died and he felt in awe to be in the Holy centre of the Christian world. The peace of mind was shattered as they left the building and returned to the noisy and dusty spice filled streets of Jerusalem.

As they headed away from the church perched on its rocky outcrop the pair were confronted by the three troublemakers. Pascal sighed heavily at seeing them. The three sneered at him and Gallien as the central man of the three remarked,

"dirtied the Holy site now have we?"

"No."

"You are with those infidels. Their evil would have rubbed off on to you." The same man replied fiercely and with disgust.

"Everything all right? Have you been inside? What is it like in there?" Qudamah, another of David's many sons, named for his now deceased friend, called out as he spotted Pascal and Gallien and not recognising the three men from their backs. He crossed to them and then realised who the three men were. He changed his mind about going to the man he thought of as his cousin but it was too late. The three troublemakers had turned round and spotted him. The one to the right shouted, "Get away from here infidel! Get out of the city! Stop eating our food Pig!"

Qudamah could stand being called everything else but getting called a pig was one step too close to his heart especially as they were dirty animals to him. With hands as fists he jumped at the three men. The three men eagerly pounced on him, crowding him.

Pascal couldn't just stand back and let his uncle's son get beaten to death. He moved into the throws of the fighting to try and even it out. Fists weren't going to work so he drew out his knife and slashed at a bare arm but then lost it as it was knocked from his hand. Gallien saw it fall and felt embarrassed that he was standing back like a coward. He stepped forward and then back again as one of the enemy was thrown out of the fight circle.

It came to a sudden halt as some of the Advocate's soldiers appeared and the three troublemakers saw them. They ran for it leaving Qudamah and Pascal battered and bruised all over. The Arab Renard dropped to the ground with one black eye already closing. Pascal was less worst for wear. He pulled Qudamah to his feet when the man held up a hand for help. With good humour he remarked, "Look at you, what a mess."

He allowed Pascal to put an arm round his waist and one of his over the Norman's shoulders especially as he had a gash in his leg.

Hadiya and Coman, her eldest, stood as fast as they could when Qudamah limped in with Pascal's help. With fear Hadiya asked, "What happened?"
Through a spilt lip Pascal replied, "These three…"

"They called me a pig." Qudamah interrupted fiercely, speaking in French for his cousin's benefit, "I could have killed them if given the chance."

"They were beating you to a pulp." Pascal exclaimed at the Arab.

"What's happened?" Qudamah's wife exclaimed in the only language she knew. She ran across to her husband and took hold of him and led him upstairs to their bedroom. Hadiya followed behind to find out how bad her son really was. Coman stayed down with the two Christians unable to believe the number of bruises on Qudamah and enquired of Pascal, "What exactly happened?"

They were talking to me and Gallien."

"Talking?"

"Insulting us, or trying to anyway. Qudamah came across and then they called him a pig. He got angry at that and just jumped on them."

"I'm not surprised since pigs are seen as dirty animals to us." Mansur calmly explained as he joined the conversation At this point Hadiya reappeared with news that Qudamah would recover, "thank you so much Pascal, you are truly Da'ud's son. I don't think anyone else would have helped Qudamah…"
Her sons all turned to stare at her. Had she really just said that Pascal was their brother? Pascal looked between them all in confusion and asked, "what did she say?"   "Brother?"

Coman frowned and instantly wondering whether this was his inheritance of a business slipping rapidly away.

Hastily she said, "you must have misheard me. I shouldn't have said anything."   "Coman, what did she say?" Pascal demanded.

Coman slowly turned to the Norman. He carefully said, "she said you were my brother."

   "Brother?"

Hadiya fled to the kitchen before anymore questions could be asked of her by anyone.

Pascal asked Coman, "where is your father?"

   "Out. Said he had to meet some long-standing customers. He'll be back later though don't know when."

Chapter 20

David was feeling merry, even slightly tipsy, as he walked through his gate. One of his long-standing Christian clients had persuaded him to have a little wine and it had been at least a year since he had had a drink. It had been a year since he had finished his small barrel that he had sneaked into the house. Yes he was a Muslim, but there was a part of him that wasn't going to give up alcohol altogether. He stopped on the threshold of his home when he saw Hadiya seated looking nervous with all of their sons around her as well as Pascal and Gallien. He realised that they must have been waiting a long time for him to return. He asked casually, trying to hide his surprise and nerves, "What is going on? Is something up?"

Hadiya rose from her seat and hurried over to him. She wrapped herself around his body. "I did a silly thing."

"What silly thing?"

"He knows." She answered cryptically.

"Who knows what?" David enquired looking completely mystified. He looked over at the men and paused at Pascal, "Oh…"

Pascal's face told him everything. It looked hurt and confused. With a heavy heart David approached his new son with his hands out in front of him palm up, "I don't know what to say…"

"Don't say anything." Snapped Pascal. As his mother wasn't here he didn't care that he was going to take it out on his supposed father, "You are despicable."

"Don't say that." Coman jumped in to defend his father. All of the sons began to shift from where Pascal stood to stand by their parents. It had quickly gone through the family vine that Pascal was a half brother and though all had been shocked they had quickly accepted that there was nothing they could do. It had all happened before they were born and their father had married one of their two mothers. It had been part of a life that their father had left behind. So, now, if this new brother was going to cause trouble for their father they would defend him.

"I can say what I want." Pascal retorted.

"Please, I can explain." David pleaded, "I can give you the letter. It is the truth."

"I don't want no sodding letter."

Looking at Pascal David saw Constance's hot blood racing through his son's veins. He felt sorrow welling up in him, this hadn't been how he wanted Pascal to find out but now it was too late.

"I could accept that you were this … this… infidel." Pascal struggled to find a word that would hurt David the most, "Mohammed worshipper, but this… this is too much. I don't care what mother may claim but I am not accepting that my father is you." Pascal was spitting the words out by the end, "I should kill you just like the pope ordered. You have no right to be living in Jerusalem. I should claim this place as my own and then burn it down because it has been tainted by bad blood, very bad blood." "That is enough!" Coman exclaimed. His hand was on the knife he always carried, "I think it is time you left this place don't you. We have shown you great generosity, welcomed you as part of the family but you are not treating us like this."

"Coman." David whispered

"No father, I am not having this. As the heir to this family I am defending it." Around Coman the other brothers were pulling knives out. A woman whimpered from upstairs where they were hiding. The grandchildren were on the balcony with the older boys and Mansur ready to come down if they were needed. Coman got a nod from the men to show they were ready to defend their family. Coman ordered Pascal, "leave here now and we won't kill you."

"Father?" Gallien asked fearfully.

"Not now Gallien." Pascal sneered, "I'll leave but don't think that I will forgive you. You are nothing now. I'm not even going to tell my mother that you live." He grabbed his son roughly by the arm and dragged him through the courtyard and out the gate.

Coman followed them to ensure they vanished down the street.

It was with a large sigh of relief that David sank on to the edge of the fountain with Hadiya still clutching his arm, "What did we do wrong?"

"You should have told him as soon as you knew." She murmured.

"That is too late now."

"I am sorry David."

He patted her on the arm, "I am not angry with you. I feel bad to say this but I am glad he has gone. There are truly no more secrets in this family although I was unaware of that one at all."

"You are going to have to explain what just happened to us father." Coman remarked, "I have a feeling he may well come back."

"We'll deal with that then, let him cool off. He has his mother's temper in him as well as mine." David remarked, "and thank you."

"You are my father and my family is what is important in my life." Coman replied

"Perhaps it is time I finally give the last of the business up to you."

"In the morning David. Now is not the time to discuss this." Hadiya pointed out.

"Yes, yes, of course. It is late, come to bed all of you, it has been a truly interesting day. Come men, you have your families to check on." David stood and led the way up the stairs where the women were now standing wide eyed.

With the departure of Pascal and Gallien nothing more was heard from them apart from the gate keeper letting Coman know that they had gone from the city as soon as the gates had opened, tearing away on two horses. The family made a silent promise amongst themselves never to mention the two Christians again and as of that moment many of the younger members became more suspicious of any friendly Christians unless they were well known clients. They hoped that the other side of the Renard family would never reappear again.

Lightning Source UK Ltd.
Milton Keynes UK
UKHW021119041022
409906UK00009B/227